Praise for *The Transcriptionist*

"Rowland seems that rare thing, the naturally gifted novelist . . . [She] deftly maps a very specific kind of urban loneliness, the inner ache of the intelligent, damaged soul who prefers the company of ideas and words to that of people . . . That urge—to make words holy—is at the heart of this novel's strange, sad beauty."   —*The Washington Post*

"*The Transcriptionist* is suffused with prescient insight into journalism, ethics, and alienation . . . A thought provoking, original work . . . Amy Rowland's debut novel could hardly have come at a more appropriate time."
                                        —*New York Journal of Books*

"*The Transcriptionist* holds many pleasures . . . [and] can be read through many lenses . . . Rowland plays with the notions of truth and reliability . . . It is the responsibility of a journalist to report the truth, but what if—Rowland asks—objective reality is a fiction? . . . Sharp and affecting."
                                        —*The New York Times Book Review*

"*The Transcriptionist* is the finest novel I've read in a while . . . [Rowland] is a deft writer with a wry sense of the fertile territory between the naturalistic and the surreal. She plays with the conventions of romance and mystery novels and leavens in a bit of philosophy when she writes about the narcotic effect of listening. But what's captivating about the novel isn't so much its plot or themes but simply the seductive city Rowland has built word by curated word. I left it reluctantly and weeks later, I still miss it. I haunted that world for a while, now it haunts me." —*Arkansas Democrat-Gazette*

"Sly and humane and with a delicate touch of surrealism, *The Transcriptionist* is a masterpiece."

—Haven Kimmel, author of *Iodine* and *A Girl Named Zippy*

"The magic of this book . . . [is that] Rowland demonstrates a gift for making mystery out of a concrete style. Paul Harding has advised writers to write 'as precisely and as lucidly and as richly' as they can about mysterious things, instead of writing with mystery and obscurity about clichés; much of *The Transcriptionist* would likely please him . . . Rowland shows her dexterity with language—her skill at nailing precisely what is mysterious about something or someone with originality, yet without preciousness . . . Remarkable." —*The Rumpus*

"This haunting, beautiful book set me thinking and dreaming about language and personality. It proves that language can make us whole. The entire book tends toward liberation, and the end is so suggestive and life-affirming, though not a typical happy ending. It's something better, something the reader can carry back into life."

—Rebecca Lee, author of *Bobcat and Other Stories*

"Original and timely." —*The Atlanta Journal-Constitution*

"Rowland's novel is best when it focuses on the daily routine of Lena's work and the perennial patterns of journalism. Her most compelling descriptions echo John Updike's sublime short story 'Pigeon Feathers' . . . Gripping." —*Ms. Magazine*

"If one had to name an antecedent for the strange, golden sheen that covers Amy Rowland's debut novel, possibly early John Cheever, with its dreamy imaginings of commuter intrigues, or beautifully cadenced, resonant verbal exchanges, would be closest. Entering the city Rowland creates, with its tightly strung dialogue and soulful, lonely citizens, is a memorable experience." —*The Boston Globe*

"A lively tale, light and enjoyable, about a sensitive, reflective and articulate soul in a fast-paced, often soulless world."
—*Minneapolis Star Tribune*

"A fine, intelligent, and emotional story."
—*Hudson Valley News*

"Rowland, a former transcriptionist for the *New York Times,* has written a strange, mesmerizing novel about language, isolation, ethics, technology, and the lack of trust between institutions and the people they purportedly serve . . . A fine debut novel about the decline of newspapers and the subsequent loss of humanity—and yes, these are related."
—*Booklist*, starred review

"[An] ambitious and fascinating debut novel . . . Disturbing and powerful; the skillfully drawn Lena may remind some readers of an existentialist hero. Recommended for fans of literary fiction."
                                                        —*Library Journal*

"Rowland's farcical approach . . . is balanced by the novel's realistic insights into journalistic integrity, the evolution of contemporary newspaper publishing, and, more broadly, the importance of genuine communication." —*Publishers Weekly*

"Unforgettable. Written with such delight, compassion, and humanity, it's newsworthy. Amy Rowland is the debut of the year."
                        —Alex Gilvarry, author of
                From the Memoirs of a Non-Enemy Combatant

"What a laser-sharp eye Amy Rowland has! From her perch in the most out-of-the-way nook in the world's most powerful paper, her heroine seems to be able to take in the whole world. This first novel is wise, beautifully written, with just the right amount of wickedness."
                        —James Magnuson, author of
                        Famous Writers I Have Known

"A haunting and provocative novel about the mysteries of life and a death, the written word, things seen and unseen, heard and forgotten. Amy Rowland's writing is compelling and masterful."   —Delia Ephron, author of *The Lion Is In*

THE TRANSCRIPTIONIST

The
Transcriptionist

A NOVEL

Amy Rowland

Algonquin Books of Chapel Hill 2015

Published by
ALGONQUIN BOOKS OF CHAPEL HILL
Post Office Box 2225
Chapel Hill, North Carolina 27515-2225

a division of
WORKMAN PUBLISHING
225 Varick Street
New York, New York 10014

First paperback edition, Algonquin Books of Chapel Hill, January 2015.
Originally published in hardcover by Algonquin Books, May 2014.
Printed in the United States of America.
Published simultaneously in Canada by Thomas Allen & Son Limited.
Design by Anne Winslow.

"There Was Earth Inside Them," from *Selected Poems and Prose of Paul Celan* by Paul Celan, translated by John Felstiner. Copyright © 2001 by John Felstiner. Used by permission of W. W. Norton & Company, Inc. Originally published in German by S. Fischer: Paul Celan, „Es war Erde in ihnen," in *Paul Celan, Die Niemandsrose*. Copyright © 1963 S. Fischer Verlag GmbH, Frankfurt am Main, Germany.

This is a work of fiction. While, as in all fiction, the literary perceptions and insights are based on experience, all names, characters, places, and incidents either are products of the author's imagination or are used fictitiously.

Library of Congress Cataloging-in-Publication Data
    Rowland, Amy, [date]
        The transcriptionist : a novel / by Amy Rowland.—First Edition.
        pages cm
    ISBN 978-1-61620-254-5 (HC)
    1. Women journalists—New York—New York City—Fiction.
    2. Lion attacks—Fiction.   3. Alienation (Social psychology)—
    Fiction.   4. Psychological fiction.   I. Title.
    PS3618.O877T73 2014
    813'.6—dc23   2013044719

    ISBN 978-1-61620-450-1 (PB)

10 9 8 7 6 5 4 3 2 1
First Paperback Edition

For Bill and Rose Rowland

"Strike through the mask!"

—CAPTAIN AHAB

THE TRANSCRIPTIONIST

CHAPTER ONE

Scientists Celebrate
Theory of Everything

No one can find it. That's the first thing. The Recording Room is on the eleventh floor, at the end of a rat-hued hallway that some workers at the newspaper have never seen; they give up on the ancient elevator, which makes only local stops with loud creaks of protest. Like New Yorkers who refuse to venture above Fourteenth Street, there are newspaper workers who refuse to go above the fourth floor for fear of being lost forever if they leave the well-lit newsroom for dark floors unknown. The newsroom, renovated, almost aglow with new computers and pale paint, seems to float in the center of the hulking institution, as if someday it will break off, drift over to Broadway, and join the Clifford and Barney balloons in the annual Macy's parade.

Occasionally, a reporter wearing cell phones, mini-keyboards, and a look of euphoric deflation finds his or her way to the eleventh floor, down the long hallway to door 1107, the Recording Room. It is an industrial door, once white, now suitably dingy, with a steel lever handle that has been known to come off and stay that way, until the proper number of union employees can be assembled for the repair.

The room is the color of old opossum or new pumice, the color of newspaper without ink. Gray. It is the room where the transcriptionist, or, in the perplexing vocabulary of the corporate world, Recording Room operator, sits alone all day with a headset and a Dictaphone and transcribes all the words that have been recorded for the *Record*.

Four dirty windows overlook Forty-Third Street and provide obstructed views of traffic and arguments, frequent parades, constant tourists, and occasional suicides. A pigeon on the window ledge presides over this scene and pecks itself incessantly, afflicted with either lice or obsessive-compulsive disorder. The windows have not been opened in three years, not since a transcriptionist pried one open and leaned out to view the body of a reporter who had jumped to his death from the roof's machine room. That transcriptionist retired soon after. Now there is one.

Today, someone has made the journey to the eleventh floor, and the Recording Room door opens. The transcriptionist looks at the metro reporter. He is handsome in a mannequin sort of way, young, tan, unlike most fluorescent-tinted reporters. The transcriptionist has always been a bit suspicious of his skin, which seems as smooth and odorless as dry ice, as if he has undergone plastination. His nervous manner makes him more bearable. Russell.

"Hi, Carol." He is one of two reporters who calls her by name and congratulates himself by repeating it often. "Thanks for the bird flu transcript. Terrifying, isn't it, Carol? Did you enjoy the interview?"

"Yes."

"You don't sound like you care, Carol."

"You didn't ask like you cared, Russell."

He shrugs, fills out the transcription log, leaves his two-tape interview about a state senator's prostatectomy, and closes the door gently with a "Many thanks, Carol."

She decided long ago not to mention that her name is Lena.

Lena is a transcriptionist, rarely mentioned in literature except to note, "The errors of copyists are the least excusable." There is basic equipment required: a headset, a Dictaphone to play the tapes that must be transcribed, and patience, a willingness to become a human conduit as the words of others enter through her ears, course through her veins, and drip out unseen through fast-moving fingertips.

While rewinding Russell's tapes, she glances at today's Metro Section: A couple charged with forcing their foster daughter to "wait on" an elderly relative as he lay dead upstairs. An article detailing the fascinating affliction of hoarding. A NYC Task Force on Hoarding has been formed. One woman quoted has a puppet problem; she buys them from a TV shopping channel. "I feel bad for them when no one else bids," she said.

Another day, another edition of the *Record,* another itemized receipt of humanity's victories and losses.

On page 3, Lena sees Russell's byline; above the story is a photo of someone who looks vaguely familiar, a middle-aged woman turned in profile, wild hair, a calm expression, eyes downcast. And the news: The woman broke into the Bronx Zoo two days ago, invaded the lions' den, and was killed. She was blind.

"Zoo officials said the woman's clothes were damp, suggesting she swam the moat. She was found lying about 40 feet from the viewing area in front of one of the dens. The employee entrances in the rear of the exhibit were locked and no keys were missing, according to zoo officials.

" 'The Bronx Zoo is very concerned about the safety of its visitors,' a zoo spokesman read from a statement. 'This incident will be studied very carefully.'

"An animal keeper discovered the body. The lions were apparently behaving strangely and would not go inside their cages to be fed.

"The animal keeper went into the lions' outdoor enclosure to try to lead them to their feeding cages. There, he found the woman, whose arms, scalp, and neck were mutilated. According to the police report, the victim suffered scratches and bite wounds over most of her body.

"The Associated Press reported that the woman had been partly devoured."

LENA STUDIES THE small picture, grainy and pale. There is something familiar about the face, but the woman has turned away from the camera and is looking off to the left, as if to protect her identity from readers of the *Record*.

She tries to remember where she has seen this woman, a woman who would swim a moat to be eaten by lions. She snaps the first tape into the Dictaphone and begins to transcribe but has difficulty concentrating. She types "prostate" and "Gleason score" and "potency" but her mind is elsewhere. When she hears the words "seminal vesicles" she lifts her foot off the pedal and pauses. She moves her foot slightly to the right and quickly presses down, then releases. The tape rewinds and she moves her foot back to the center of the pedal and presses: "seminal vesicles." Yes, that's what he said. It's enough to make one feel sorry for politicians; even their seminal vesicles are subject to discussion. But then Russell asks if it's true that the senator urged the president to send the military into a Binghamton suburb to arrest terrorism suspects. "It would seem to be a clear violation of posse comitatus," Russell says. "Posse comitatus," the senator shouts. "I'm sure the president did not violate posse co- mitatus. What is posse comitatus? It sounds vaguely por- nographic and I'm sure the president had nothing to do with it."

She closes her eyes, then opens them and focuses on the telephones across the room. Three black phones are mounted on a panel and linked to recorders with electri- cal umbilical cords so that reporters can call in to dictate their stories. The bulk of work these days is the tran- scription of long interviews that are folded into stories like the one she is typing now, although calls come in sporadically, unpredictably. There is a red light above the telephone that flashes with an incoming call. She imag- ines this to be like the red button of Samuel Beckett's tele- phone, although he used his to exclude incoming calls, which, alas, the transcriptionist cannot. And anyway, these phones are not for transmitting literature; they are news lines, dedicated to the who, the what, the when, the where, and sometimes, perhaps, the why. To talk on these phones, the transcriptionist must press a button on the receiver and hold it down while she speaks. But once she has taken the initial, necessary information (caller, desk, time, location, slug), she rarely presses the button again. This makes for a cleaner transcript because if the button on the receiver is not pressed and the transcriptionist does not speak, there is no background noise on the tape. She is a transcriptionist, but also a gatekeeper for background noise.

She continues typing about the politician's prostate, and her mind drifts from Samuel Beckett's telephone to the blind woman to butterflies. This may seem a strange progression to someone who has not been a transcriptionist. But transcriptionists know that typing someone else's words encourages a mysterious progression of thoughts, as in dreams. So, Coetzee, Nabokov, Saramago—butterfly men all. She had cried on the R train once while reading of the rasp of butterfly teeth. What was the passage?

"The scratch of ant-feet, the rasp of butterfly teeth, the tumbling of dust."

In her daydream, as her fingers continue to move silently over the keyboard, Lena already sees the grave of the blind woman who was devoured by lions. It is in a potter's field; small white bricks serve as markers, row upon row, like long lines of white hyphens where names should be recorded. That is what will happen if the woman's body is not claimed. It will not be enough for her, but that is what will be done.

While transcribing, Lena recites things to herself. Recitation is a habit she has always found soothing, silently reciting whatever passage occurs as her fingers play the keys. But recently the recitation does not seem to stop. She awakens in the morning with someone else's words, someone else's thoughts, ribboning around her brain. And while she is transcribing, she recites, without realizing, things she has learned from transcribing stories and interviews, mixed in with the flotsam of dreams until she does not know anymore what is real and what is *Record*: That the world is made of two shapes, the doughnut and the sphere. That Newton lived his whole life within 150 miles and died a virgin. That there are nine billion pieces of candy corn.

She closes her eyes and sees the blind woman's face. Her job is to remember voices and she has gradually stopped remembering faces. But not this one.

Russell opens the door halfway. "Hey, Carol, how's the transcript coming?"

She nods.

"Soon?"

She nods again and sighs as the door closes. Once

again a politician's prostate must take priority—an unfortunate but common truth.

The telephone rings; the red light flashes. She removes the headset and crosses the room, picks up the receiver of the first phone on the panel while simultaneously pressing "record" on the Dictaphone.

"Recording Room."

"Hi, this is John Miller with a lead for the science desk."

"OK, John, where are you calling from?"

"Aspen."

She records the time and location of the call on the phone log.

"What's the slug?"

"Slug it Theory of Everything."

"OK, go ahead when you're ready."

She watches the tape wind slowly around the spool and listens for the dictation to begin.

"Physicists gathered in Aspen to celebrate the twentieth anniversary of string theory comma the so hyphen called theory of everything comma which they admit that they still cannot test stop."

Lena gently hangs the receiver next to the recorder, on a plastic hook that keeps the call from being disconnected. She returns to her desk, replaces her headphones, and continues with the prostatectomy.

Six minutes later, while she is standing by the panel rewinding the Theory of Everything, the phone rings.

"Hi, this is John Miller calling from Aspen. I have a lead for the science desk. Slug it Theory of Nothing."

Lena presses the button that allows her to speak on the recording line. "Hi, John. I thought you just called from Aspen with the lead for the Theory of Everything."

There is a loud curse on the other end. "I did. Can you believe it? The Theory of Nothing people, not to be outdone by the Theory of Everything people, are holding their conference in a hotel across the street. So I'm running back and forth between the two, glancing up at the banner in the banquet room to remember if I'm at Everything or Nothing."

She laughs.

"Don't laugh. These damn physicists. They've got more splinter groups than Al Qaeda in Mesopotamia."

"But aren't the theory of everything and the theory of nothing the same thing?"

"Probably."

"Maybe I could just play the Theory of Everything lead backward and I'd have the Theory of Nothing."

There is silence on the line.

"It was a joke, John. Go ahead with the Theory of Nothing."

"OK. Lead. Physicists gathered in Aspen to celebrate the theory of nothing stop. Physicists concede that in technical terms a nothing is really a something dash the energy in empty space stop. But that did not prevent the group here from celebrating the anniversary of nothing as the beginning of everything comma or what one of the cosmologists here called the deeper nothing stop."

AT SEVEN O'CLOCK she calls the news desks for a "goodnight," or permission to leave, first foreign, then national, then metro.

"Hi, this is the Recording Room calling for a goodnight."

The news clerk puts the phone down to ask the desk head's permission and then comes back on the line.

"Good night, Recording."

She repeats this with the other desks and is given the goodnight from people who know her name only as "Recording." It is a holdover from years ago, when there were twenty-four transcriptionists and they had to be available for breaking news and frantic phone calls late into the night. The young news clerks seem to enjoy this mysterious nightly ritual of a voice somewhere in the belly of the *Record* asking to go home. It is evidence of something, of tradition and history, for which they otherwise have no use.

A few times in the past four years she has been asked to call again an hour or two hours or three hours later for the goodnight: on September 11, and after the American Airlines flight to the Dominican Republic crashed in Queens. When the space shuttle *Columbia* was destroyed she was called in on a weekend. She stays late to transcribe big speeches, the State of the Union address, presidential debates. On those nights a news clerk is sent up to the Recording Room to cut five- and eight-minute sections of tape while Lena transcribes.

She turns out the lights and takes the phones off the hooks so that calls will bounce to the overnight machine. She locks the door, then unlocks it again. The newspaper is in its hanging file folder by the door—a week's worth of *Record*—and she removes today's paper and cuts out the article on the blind woman, which she folds and puts in her pocket.

On the sidewalk she hesitates, choosing her route home. East on Forty-Third, then down Fifth Avenue? Sometimes she walks down Broadway and east on Forty-Second Street. This is her masochistic route, letting Forty-Second Street overwhelm her; she seeks the garish sights of Times Square, where pedestrians take on the glow of the afterlife.

Not today; she turns east on Forty-Third, and the fifty-cent lady steps from the shadows of the building. She wears loose-laced brogans with no socks, a long pleated skirt, and, though it is eighty-five degrees, a stained men's trench coat in which she resembles a distraught Electra in her slain father's clothing. "Fifty cents!" she cries, exclaiming rather than questioning. She never speaks any other words, but her tone indicates that she recognizes the newspaper workers who pass her every day. It is as if the exact amount owed and denied is being recorded and must be answered for on that day when all one's failures and shortcomings are tallied. Lena places two quarters in the woman's lined palm and walks away. When she first began working at the paper, the woman shouted, "Twenty-five cents!" and it depresses her to think that she has been a transcriptionist long enough for inflation to influence the homeless.

Across Broadway the NYPD sign blinks in neon above its small metal shack like an old-fashioned diner in a desert. She continues past the Woodstock Hotel, where dapper old men sit with a boom box, past the Japanese grocery with a bulletin board advertising apartments, language lessons, and a painting, *Madonna of the Harpies*. She turns south at Sixth Avenue, then east on Forty-Second, past Bryant Park with its monuments to Goethe and Gertrude, who squats like a cranky, sleepy Buddha near the lawn. The lawn where, according to a vague but shocking park association note, "for a brief period the city buried hundreds of poor." Perhaps a few shards of anonymous bones still lie beneath the grassy lawn where democracy prevails on sunny days, when the rich and poor remove their shoes and lie side by side, their faces toward the sun.

When she turns right on Fifth Avenue, the library lions Patience and Fortitude provide familiar comfort.

In contrast to Gertrude Stein's statue, they recline with feline grace, unflappable and serene.

It is here, in front of the library filled with names and words of those long dead, that Lena thinks again of the blind woman and remembers where she saw her.

It was on the bus.

Three days ago she had a migraine, and here in front of the library is where she succumbed. With migraines, her vision sometimes becomes static, reflecting still images instead of moving ones. Of all the interesting and bizarre experiences of New York, seeing the city frozen instead of in motion is the most unsettling. So when the downtown bus stopped, Lena got on and sat beside a woman who had a braille book on her lap. The woman could have been in her forties or her sixties. She had an oval, open face, striking because it had not settled into the Manhattan mask of predator or prey. Lena focused on the woman to fight nausea and steady her vision. The bus lurched and motion returned. Are the blind immune to motion sickness? she wondered.

The woman's hands were lined; ropy veins ended at large knuckles. Elongated fingers moved with fluidity over the raised letters. Lena thought she would make it home if she focused on the fingers. She swallowed, realized she was quietly repeating a phrase to herself as had become her habit. "Truth beareth away the victory," from the library's facade. The blind woman's fingers stopped; she turned and seemed to see Lena, who blushed and looked down at her hands in confusion. When she glanced up again the woman was still turned toward her with a rueful half smile.

"What are you reading?" Lena asked.

"The Veldt."

"Ray Bradbury?"

"You know it?"

"It affected me greatly as a teenager."

"Yes," the woman said, smiling, as if she were considering a secret, and Lena realized how mysterious smiles are when the eyes are dead. "Yes. But it's different now."

"How?"

"It's quite blunt, but still chilling. When the man finds his wallet that the lions have been chewing—"

"And when he and his wife recognize their own screams."

"Yes," the woman said. "That's the part that affects me most, the couple recognizing their own voices."

Lena tried to imagine the blind woman screaming and then silently chastised herself for wondering if blind people scream. Of course they could, physically, but for some reason she couldn't imagine it.

"Would you recognize your own?" the woman said quietly.

Lena's head was pulsing with pain. She told herself that the woman was probably not being as cryptic as she seemed, that it was the distorted dreaminess of a migraine. "I'm not much of a screamer."

"It's like murder. We all have the capacity, but we don't all have the desire."

Lena was too surprised to respond, and she flinched as the bus bounced over a bump. She didn't think she had made any sound, but the woman asked, "Are you OK?"

"I have a migraine, it makes me unsteady."

The woman nodded. "I used to have them, but then I went blind and was cured."

"Hmm," Lena said, because it felt impolite to laugh.

"Here, may I try something? Give me your hand."

"You're not going to read my palm, are you?" Lena asked, trying to hide her discomfort.

The woman smiled and reached out, grasping Lena's hand as if she had perfect vision. "Oh, I know," the woman said. "You hate mysticism."

"Well, then, maybe you are a mind reader."

The woman lightly stroked her hand, and Lena was too stunned to move. But I'm not the hand-holding type, she almost said, but didn't. She tried to remember the last time she had held hands with anyone. It wasn't with her last lover, Richard. They were neither of them hand-holders and they had understood that about each other. She had been out with exactly one man since then. On the third date, he not only held her hand while walking down the street but *swung* it back and forth. She had broken things off with him the same night.

"The world goes by my cage but no one sees me."

"Pardon?"

"I'm looking inside your cage," the woman said. "I see words."

"I'm a transcriptionist for the *Record*."

She glanced around to see if anyone had noticed that she was holding a woman's hand, but all the passengers were absorbed with palm-size screens or lost in a tired-eyed commuter's coma.

The woman tapped her hand gently, in a reassuring, comforting way.

"I'm a court reporter," she said. "Voices coursing through our veins. You can't live that way forever, not people like us."

"What kind of people are we?"

The woman lightly pressed the web of skin between Lena's thumb and index finger. The two of them sat silently for a full minute or more, and Lena realized that although she still had a headache, she didn't feel as dizzy.

"Be careful what you listen to," the woman said. "Be careful what you hear."

"But that's my job. I have to listen to everything. That's what I do."

"We can't keep up with the suffering of others. We have to close ourselves off. How else can we survive?" The bus was close to Twenty-Third Street and Lena stood abruptly. "I have to go. This is my stop." "Be careful," the woman said. "You live a dangerous life." Then she began to read again. Lena watched her fingers flit across the white page, the words concealed to all but the blind. She wanted to say something more but she didn't know with what words, so she said thank you and got in line to exit.

". . . that roar which lies on the other side of silence." Lena wasn't sure she had heard right and looked back, but the woman had turned her head toward the window and her expression was inscrutable. All went still and static again; there was no movement, no sound. She thought of Lot's wife, turning back, turning to salt stone, but in Lena's version, stranger still, it was New York that was turning to stone as she watched, helpless.

Someone behind her said, "Hey," and gave her a slight push. "Go if you're going. I got to get off."

The pain came roaring back, behind her eyes, pushing to exit through her ears, a stormy sea was in her head, and she stumbled down the bus steps to the street.

She stepped on someone's foot, and vomit rose along with apology in her throat. She swallowed them both and for a terrible moment she could not see. She made it to a metal trash can on the corner and heaved with a violence that shocked her. No one seemed to notice, and she eventually shuffled to a bench in Madison Square Park near the statue of Chester Arthur. The man who became president only after the assassination of another stood before his throne-like bronze chair and she wanted to tell him that he could be seated.

CHAPTER TWO

Hearing Is the Last Sense
to Abandon the Dying

Tonight, she is still thinking of the blind woman as she approaches the Salvation Army residence on Gramercy Park. The Parkside Evangeline, where "many advantages of home are provided for young women of moderate income." Some of the residents have not been young in quite a long time, but Lena tries not to think about this because she is terrified of becoming one of them, a woman who never leaves.

She enters Parkside, passes the reception desk, where the old widow, Mrs. Pelletier (don't call her "Ms."), sits guarding her imagined treasures, the residents' chastity. If a man steps foot past her Plexiglas lookout post, she flings her hand up like a stop sign and cries out, "Stop! Go no further!" Lena sometimes silently adds, "Stop! I am a temple of the Holy Ghost!" like the girl in Flannery O'Connor's story.

Two meals a day are paid for, whether one eats them or not. It's not as depressing as it looks, Lena tells herself, standing in the dining room's entrance and looking at the faded green-and-rose-print carpet. Lots of young women smile and pair off and eat with gusto. But she feels most out of place when peering into the dining room, where plastic carnations in milk-colored vases line long tables under ceiling fans that whir like ancient coffee percolators. It is in the dining room that the two groups of residents are most distinct. There are the elderly ladies, as they are called, the ones who remain permanently in this place of limbo. And there are the women in their twenties, many of them visiting from other countries, who use Parkside as a kind of youth hostel. Lena fits into neither category, though she comforts herself that at thirty-three she is still closer in age to the younger group.

She looks at tonight's menu posted by the door: glazed meat, always the glaze, apricot glaze, sweet glaze, cloying glaze. She cannot. The elevator delivers her to the "solarium" on the seventeenth floor, a rectangular green room with a fuzzy-screen TV, two rickety exercise bikes, and folding tables and chairs designed for reunions and church revivals. Glass doors lead to the sun deck, a bare, concrete area surrounded by an eye-level wall.

Restless, she decides to take the stairs down to her room. Two girls are in the stairwell, hanging out the window. The one with a Mickey Mouse T-shirt turns with anticipation.

"Come here," she says, motioning with her hands. "See that rooftop over there, the one with the trees and the glass door to the penthouse? That's Julia Roberts's place. We saw her come out on the terrace! She was talking on the phone!"

"Then she went back inside!" cries the second girl.

"But we're waiting for her to come back out!" the first girl says. "She might!"

"Wait till I tell my mom I can watch Julia Roberts's apartment. She'll just die!"

"Isn't this city just neat?"

"Yeah," Lena says. She turns to descend the stairs. "Don't fall out the window."

They both laugh. "Of course not!"

"I wonder if she'll see us!" the girl's voice echoes down the stairwell.

LENA'S ROOM IS small but furnished; it has a private bathroom, with handrails in the shower. The desk with attached bookshelves tips over when she stands on a chair and pulls a book down too quickly. There is a radio and a squat beige telephone but no television.

Lying on the bed, she pushes against the wall with her feet and stares at the ceiling. The *Middlemarch* passage that the blind woman quoted floats before her eyes, as if she is transcribing for the author and watching the words appear above. "If we had a keen vision and feeling of all ordinary human life, it would be like hearing the grass grow and the squirrel's heart beat, and we should die of that roar which lies on the other side of silence." She closes her eyes tight, then opens them, but the words remain, creeping across the white ceiling. She cannot escape them. They unwind slowly like a parasitic worm, taking up more and more of her brain. It reminds her of African river blindness—which she had transcribed an article on last summer—when the nematode worm finds a host in the unsuspecting victim's body and grows and grows until it needs more space and comes out through the eyes. "No," she says, and she hurries from the room.

At the front desk, Mrs. Pelletier guards something even rarer than chastity—four keys to Gramercy Park. Surprisingly, there is usually at least one key available. Lena signs her name on the xeroxed form in the black Book of Keys. After being reminded to return within an hour, she crosses the street and unlocks the park gate.

New Yorkers, who famously pride themselves on not looking at people no matter how famous or outrageous they are, always turn their heads at the sound of the gate opening into Gramercy Park. Someone has the key, the key! to the exclusive oasis, the small patch of gated grass and gravel.

Lena opens the iron gate and slips inside, heading toward the statue of John Wilkes Booth's brother, the actor Edwin Booth, as Hamlet. "Alas, poor ghost!" she says, giving him a pat. He is surrounded by a gravel oval running the length of the park, where key holders can stroll partly hidden by the trees. The trees, like the lovely London plane with its mottled trunk, wear name tags, as if they were corporate professionals at a convention: "Hi! My name is Ohio buckeye." Lena loops the park twice and settles on a south-facing bench.

Two gray-haired women in floral dresses gather their things and leave the park arm in arm, the one with swollen ankles supported by her companion. They have been reading, sitting on separate benches. A breeze reveals the dark elastic bands at the top of their nude knee-highs.

People are leaving the park; it is growing dark. The gray light of evening descends like a silken net under the trees. The faux gas lamps come on with an electrical twitch. It is the time of day that belongs to twilight, quick footsteps, doors and gates clanging closed, and the very young and very old disappearing inside. The changing of the guard: the old and young retreat to their buildings, the workers advance from theirs.

Parkside residence is quiet when she returns, and she is scolded for keeping the park key twenty extra, undocumented minutes. But she is so quiet and takes the scolding so obediently that Mrs. Pelletier removes her pointed glasses, worn so long they have come back in style, unbeknownst to her, and says that she remembers losing track of time in the park a long, long time ago. Her voice is all wistfulness and longing, yet it is clear that she would no more take one of the exclusive keys in her charge and let herself into the park than she would allow a male to enter a resident's room. Lost hours in the park belong to a place she cannot access, even though the land itself lies just across the street.

"Mrs. Pelletier," Lena says softly.

Mrs. Pelletier snaps the eyeglasses from their dangling chain, pushes them forcefully across her nose, and makes a pointed, deliberate X beside Lena's name in the Book of Keys. She prints in big capital letters, "LATE," and closes the thick black binder. "Punctuality is paramount, Ms. Respass. Tardiness is unacceptable in the *real* world."

AS SHE LIES in bed, unable to sleep, Lena thinks of the blind woman and the city's potter's fields, the one on Hart Island, which can only be visited by special permission, and the one that used to lie under the Forty-Second Street library, under the grand facade and the words "Truth beareth away the victory."

Sleepily, she tries to remember the origin of the quote; it was from the book of Esdras, Ezra. She remembers because of the unusual sentence. "Women are strongest: but above all things, truth beareth away the victory." Memorization had been her companion in her lonely southern childhood. Her father was a farmer and a minister, and when he discovered that she had a skill for remembering, he had her memorize verses to open his sermon on Sundays. It began as her companion and became her curse. Language was a game, that was how it started, a game between her and her father, the only one they ever played. She was a teenager before she comprehended what her father and his congregation believed.

That was the first betrayal. They took her into church before she had the power of speech, when she was still drooling and had bows velcroed to her nearly naked head, and passed her up and down the pew, letting the ruffles on her underpants show. All the while they were talking, telling her things, how things were, how things are, how things will be. And even though they could conjugate all the tenses, they understood only the past. When she found herself on the far side of a lonely chasm, she still believed in language. She thought that she could throw away God and keep language, that words would save her.

When she left for college, thanks to a teaching scholarship that she ended up not honoring, life opened up for a while, and she built a student life that felt almost normal. Since that was the only normalcy she knew, she went on to graduate school in New York and settled on a thesis exploring power and domination in the novels of George Eliot.

She had not spoken to her father in two years when he died, and for a few months she almost forgot he was dead as she continued with her research and withdrew from the small social circle she had acquired with doggedness. Then she began to miss seminars and would find herself sitting for hours in Riverside Park staring into the Hudson. The end of her academic career came at exactly two o'clock on a Tuesday in a diner on Broadway. A Salvadoran waiter had approached her table and asked, "Are you reading the Bible?" She looked up from the red leather-bound copy of *Middlemarch* she had bought for five dollars at Strand. "No, why?" The waiter looked forlorn. "You looked like you might be," he said, "but girls here never are."

For the first time, she looked around the room at the diners eating scrambled eggs and cheeseburgers, at a busboy flirting with a waitress, at a pudgy toddler putting a french fry up his nostril, and she looked down at the book that she now studied instead of enjoyed, the book that she was trying to put between herself and the world as she retreated into the academic tower.

She had relinquished religion, but just like the others in her father's flock, she led a life of submission.

A week later she left the program and took a job in classified advertising at the *Record*. She was very good at helping customers squeeze their copy into the five-line minimum, which made her popular with advertisers but not with her advertising managers, who hastily recommended her for the Recording Room opening, lauding her "excellent listening and typing skills." And so she locked herself up in another tower, one she has not even tried to escape.

That is how she came to spend her days alone in a room transcribing the words of others. She still relies on quotes she has memorized to converse with people, especially when she feels awkward or shy, though she talks with fewer and fewer people as time passes.

THE BLIND WOMAN announces herself in the dark, like the projected image from old filmstrips they used to show in grade school. She is frozen except for her fingers, which move across the empty expanse, stroking the invisible letters to bring them to life. She is a transcriptionist, too, Lena thinks, except the words enter her fingertips where they exit mine.

She closes her eyes, and the blind woman's face merges with the immovable faces of the library lions, then the faces of the lions at their terrible task, ripping away the woman's limbs, her fingers.

And then he appears. Her own devourer, the one who has followed her everywhere for years, elusive and yet ever close, he always comes.

When she was thirteen, the summer her mother died, a mountain lion came to the farming town where she lived. Or at least he was rumored to be in the area.

Ernest Cutler had been driving back from Jamesville when he saw the cat crouching by the ditch along Highway 32. He said the cat was so still he thought it might be dead and he kept driving, but then he decided to circle back. When he got to the ditch, the cat was gone.

Then Ernestine Baker swore that he—everyone called him "he" from the beginning—had been rooting through her trash barrel. She had shot at him from the bathroom window with her pearl-handled Beretta, but he was too far away and it was too dark.

Lena had learned in school that the eastern cougar was extinct and had not been recorded in the Southeast since the 1930s, but reports of sightings persisted, because like so many things there, a good story solidified the existence of things unseen.

Ghost cat. Catamount. Puma. Painter. Panther. Mountain lion. Cougar.

She had memorized all the names it had been given over the years. Her teacher said that the cat was known by different names in different areas and that it was once common across the continent and from southern Canada to the tip of South America.

SHE AWAKENS, THRASHING sweaty sheets, and lies in the dark. Sleep will not come, and she flips the pillow over, searching in vain for a cool spot. Lying on her back, she hears the unmistakable sound. First there is the click. Then the sound of tape slowly winding around its spool. Her fingers tense, as if poised above a keyboard. She listens.

"Hearing is the last sense to abandon the dying," says the voice on the invisible tape.

"No!" She jerks up in bed, looking around the room. Perhaps it was a daydream.

CHAPTER THREE

Power Failure Causes New York Blackout; Thousands Stranded

Morning in the Recording Room. She checks the overnight machine; no one called. She takes an unfinished tape from the rack. It is a long, boring magazine interview on the millionaire's dating club (for women, "tough love, internal makeover, hair straightener"; for men, "the penis does the picking") that she has two days to turn around and is not eager to finish. She looks out the window at the frantically scratching pigeon, then closes the blinds and sits down at the desk, which is just large enough for the boxy computer and, on her left, the Dictaphone, a dictionary, and *The Record Manual of Style*.

She opens today's paper and reads, turning the pages and trying not to get ink on her fingers. In Mexico a woman gave herself a C-section with a kitchen knife. Britain is running out of burial space. Twenty-one women died in a stampede for free saris in India, at an event sponsored by a politician.

She sits down at the Dictaphone and presses the foot pedal. There is empty time on side B of the tape before the interview with the millionaire matchmaker continues, and she listens, concentrating for the first word. The silence continues, but she hears something, a humming almost. There is a story about John Cage in a studio to record 4'33", four minutes and thirty-three seconds of silence. He said he heard two sounds in the silence, one high, one low; he said the high sound was his central nervous system and the low his blood circulating. She doesn't know whether the story is true, or whether it was even about John Cage. She tells herself lots of stories when sitting alone with the headsets, but she no longer trusts which parts are true.

"Let's wait a minute," the reporter says on the tape. The interview is at a restaurant, and a group nearby is singing "Happy Birthday." The reporter pauses the interview but does not turn off the recorder, and Lena looks around the Recording Room as she listens to strangers sing a song that sounds haunting in her secluded room.

Ten minutes later, she is in her transcriptionist trance and jumps when the phone rings.

"This is Katheryn Keel," the recording line voice announces, "calling from Baghdad with a lead for the foreign desk."

"OK, Katheryn, go ahead when you're ready."

"Do you know who this is?"

"You said it's Katheryn Keel."

"Yes, but I mean, do you know who I am? As in Katheryn Keel, the senior foreign correspondent, Katheryn Keel, the first reporter to embed with the Marines."

"OK, Katheryn Keel. If you want to dictate something, I'll transcribe it."

"I just want to make sure you give it priority. And don't send it to the foreign desk. Send it straight to Ralph. I'll give you his e-mail. And this is just the lead. I'll call back with the adds."

"OK."

"Slug it Baghdad Foot. A suicide bomber blew himself up today in the center of Baghdad's busiest market stop. It was two in the afternoon and the market was full of women and children stop. Authorities put the death toll at thirty-seven but it is expected to rise stop. Two hours after the blast comma blood and clothes and shoes lay in a heap with vegetables and glass stop. A charred foot comma unattached to anything comma lay in the dirt stop. Graph.

"A witness said he blacked out comma came to comma tried to move comma quote and a voice in my head told me not to look down stop end quote. Then he realized he was stumbling over bodies stop."

Lena types "bodies" and the recording line rings again. She runs around her desk to the phone panel by the door, expecting Katheryn with the first add to her story.

"Recording Room."

"Hi, this is Maggie Bradley with the wedding column."

"Where are you calling from, Maggie?"

"Oh, what? You mean this isn't a recording? I thought you were a machine."

"No."

"Sorry."

"Happens all the time. So where are you calling from?"

"West Palm Beach. This is a rush and the society desk needs it right away, attention Tom Richardson. Can you rush it?"

"I'll try."

"Well, can you or can't you?"

"Sure, Maggie. I'll rush the wedding column."

"Great. And I have a note to the editor that I'll dictate at the beginning. Please put it in bold."

Lena puts the phone down and finishes the Baghdad

lead—"quote We would go comma quote a man standing on the sidewalk said stop. Quote But where would
we go and how would we get there question mark end
quote"—and begins the wedding story. Maggie does not
give punctuation.

Lena transcribes:

"Note to editor: Tom, this is what happens when you
put a reporter on society coverage. I want a real beat,
Tom. Remember that when you read this. A real beat!"

"OK. Vows column. Elizabeth, the daughter of the former finance minister of a South American country, and
Drake, the son of Victor V. W. Blankoff, met at a polo
match in Brazil. They plan to travel the world for a year
and then make a documentary film.

" 'We want to take our time,' the bride said, her eyes
as blue as a Tiffany's box, 'and find a deserving subject.
We're going to start doing research right away, on our
honeymoon safari in Africa. I can't wait to go to Africa.'

"The groom, twenty-nine, is a retired hedge fund
founder and a buyer of polo horses and conceptual art.
The bride is a photographer whose work has been ex-
hibited in the flagship stores of Hermès and Ferragamo.
'Please note that it's the flagship stores,' the bride said.
'I wouldn't want people to think my work was being
shown at a ratty-ass mall.' "

The recording line rings and Lena rushes to the phone.
It's the first add from Baghdad. She hurries back to her

desk and pops the wedding tape out of the Dictaphone, then rushes back to the recording line and starts a second tape recording so that she can start transcribing the first tape right away.

"Authorities say the head of the suicide bomber has been recovered but he has not been identified stop. Women in black wailed in the demolished market stop. One woman stood in the middle of the road in a daze holding a shoe that she said belonged to her son stop. Graph."

She finishes with Baghdad and then it's back to Elizabeth and Drake.

"The bride hired Bardley Buckley, a New York designer, to create a winter scene from *Doctor Zhivago* inside the Ritz-Carlton with three hundred white-painted trees and forty thousand white orchids . . ."

Lena sends the transcripts, removes the headset, and rubs her eyes. She walks to the window, where the sudden opening of the blinds startles the pigeon.

"Jump," she says. She struggles to raise the window so that the bird can hear her better. Stuck. She bangs it with her hand. Finally it opens and she leans out. "Jump! You're a bird. Go on."

He puts his claw down in defiance and looks at her with pigeon eyes.

"It's not lice, is it, pigeon? A case of OCD, maybe?"

Someone coughs behind her and she turns.

"Hi, Carol."

"Hi, Russell."

"I wondered if you finished the interview."

"Of course. I e-mailed it to you."

"Oh," he says. "Great." He looks behind her at the window. "Were you talking to yourself just now?"

"Oh." She shrugs and wonders whether it is better to confess to talking to herself or to a pigeon. "Yes, guess so."

He smiles. "Interesting day?"

"I just transcribed a story about a Baghdad bombing from Katheryn Keel."

They both smile at the name. Katheryn Keel looks good on paper and television. She is a legend, the ex-wife of Ralph, the executive editor, and a foreign reporter who by all accounts was fearless until false bravado got in the way and hardened into self-certitude. It was true, she was unafraid of corrupt territory, be it a country or a source. She has made her way through both kinds.

"So, do you have an interview for me?"

"What? Oh, no. I just . . . " He looks down at the tapes in their plastic cases, stacked horizontally in the shabby cardboard box beside the phone panel. He runs his fingers along the plastic case spines, in a childlike movement, like a boy running his hand along a fence. He glances up at her, and the movement takes on new meaning as he seems to wink, but she tells herself he is just adjusting his glasses.

"Did you come to pick up your tape from yesterday?"

"Right, yes."

"Here it is."

"Thanks." Without turning, he reaches behind him, groping for the door handle, which comes off in his hand.

"Oh. That happens sometimes."

"Gee." He glances from her face to the handle in his hand.

"A man will be imprisoned in a room with a door that's unlocked and opens inward, as long as it does not occur to him to pull rather than push."

She sticks her fingers in the hole where the lever was and wiggles her fingers. "Except in this case, it's more about being imprisoned until your hand becomes the handle."

"What?"

"Oh, I think this door handle looks like one Wittgenstein designed. He planned a house once, for his sister, and it took him a year to design the door handle. His sister admired the house but she could not live in it."

"You read Wittgenstein?"

"A long time ago, in grad school."

"You went to grad school?"

"I went to grad school, but I dropped out."

"Do you always quote philosophers to unsuspecting journalists?"

"What? No, I guess quoting people is a transcriptionist's hazard."

"I don't think anyone has interviewed Wittgenstein lately."

She can feel the red streak of embarrassment race across her cheeks and down to her chest.

"I'm sorry. Quoting, it's a habit. I don't get a lot of visitors here. My conversation skills are rusty."

"It's OK. I didn't mean—well," he says, putting the door handle on the transcription log, "I better go."

"Russell, remember that story you wrote a few days ago, about the woman at the zoo?"

"Yeah, sad story. What about it?"

"I saw the woman before she died. We were on the same bus, and I can't get her out of my mind."

"What are the chances you would have met her?"

"That's what I keep telling myself. Do you know anything else about her?"

"No, I had no time, the deadline was tight, and there wasn't much information except that a blind woman had been eaten by lions. It was really a wire story but it was so strange we had to cover it."

"Do you still think about it? Are there stories that are hard to let go?"

"There's always a new story."

"It never bothers you, that it's so ephemeral?"

"What's not? Yesterday, today, tomorrow. Amen. Bye, Carol."

She opens her mouth to correct him but he is already gone. At the window, she says to the pigeon, "My name isn't Carol." She takes a package of crackers from her desk drawer and puts them out on the ledge after breaking them into small pieces.

SHE IS AT the deli on Forty-Third and Sixth buying a container of already curdled cottage cheese for lunch when the lights flicker, then go dark. She walks outside; lights are out around the block. People spill onto the sidewalk and look around dazed. Traffic slows and angry voices sound from taxis; arms and heads are thrust out open windows. The horns begin, then the chorus of voices like fire through a sun-scorched field. "Can you get a connection?" pedestrians ask as they lift their cell phones and stumble among others who are also lifting their cell phones toward the indifferent sun.

Disembodied voices utter fragments to the air, a mass of impotent humanity.

"It's a blackout."

"Can you get a connection?"

"It's like a dream."

"It's like a movie."

"Can you get a connection?"

"Traffic lights are out. No lights in Times Square. Looks like a blackout."

"A blackout?"

Lena joins the hapless parade threading through Times Square. On Broadway a woman in a floral hat stops her. "How long does this last?"

"I don't know," Lena says.

"I told you we should have gone to Niagara Falls," the woman says to what can only be her middle-aged son, a florid man flanked by two florid children.

Lena continues across Broadway; Times Square is eerie in the natural light, without ticker tapes or flashing billboards or traffic lights. The pedestrians seem even smaller as they cross the square, blinking in the summer sun, like disaster victims stumbling through a steamy concrete purgatory.

The *Record*'s elevators are out, so Lena trudges up eleven dark flights of stairs—lit only with yellow glow tape—to the Recording Room, where her boss, Ned, awaits, a pear-faced man with plastered-down hair.

"Lena. Where were you?"

"Lunch."

She rarely sees her boss. He works on another floor and supervises a group of people who do something in shifts and speak in acronyms. It is a mystery to both of them why he is her manager.

He swipes at the sweat on his bulby forehead. "I guess you know there's been a blackout. It's citywide. We're on generators and the newsroom is looking for people to take dictation over the phone."

"Do you want me to go?"

"Do you want to go?" he asks carefully. He has been through enough middle-management training to know how to talk to union employees, following the *Record*'s dominant management style, based on the government model of strategic ambiguity (keep them in the dark, and give them light only as absolutely necessary). There are two management styles at the *Record* and a constant struggle between the two: the advocates of ambiguity, and the supporters of the more aggressive "mushroom model" (keep them in the dark, and feed them shit). The managers pride themselves on knowing which model they follow, because the workers sometimes have difficulty telling the difference.

"Sure, Ned. I'll go."

"I don't know about overtime, you know, if it would be the newsroom's responsibility or the—"

"Ned, it's fine. I'll go."

"Great. When you get to the newsroom, ask for Boris Hackney."

• • •

Journey to the Center

She follows the stairwell glow tape to the fourth floor. The newsroom has two levels with a central staircase, the stairway to heaven, where newspaper gods dole out assignments and publisher's awards. Heaven dwellers are served snacks every afternoon, and if disaster somewhere in Manhattan causes newsroom employees to work late into the night, a full dinner is catered. *Record* readers might find a more accurate account of New York City catastrophes by viewing the buffet table in the newsroom: political debates and local elections—pizza; tornado in Brooklyn—burritos; terrorism in Manhattan and presidential elections—Virgil's Barbecue.

The newsroom is more updated than anywhere else in the century-old building but still looks like a benign government agency in a bad budget cycle. Lena looks around the beige, fluorescent-lit office and wishes for a touch of squalor. The room thrums with neuroses but there is no seediness; Miss Lonelyhearts replaced by the Ethicist who does not invoke God or Art or Sex but gives sanitized, secular advice.

A gleeful group is huddled, having discovered a clerk's memoir in his backpack. Several investigative reporters slump unhappily around a radio, specialists sidelined by the trauma team.

Lena is always disappointed anew at the room, where

instead of bald, bespectacled men typing with one heavy hand and reaching into the drawer for the bourbon bottle with the other, it is the usual corporate subdivision: well-medicated activity, soundless keypads, and clusters of low-partitioned cubicles in a rectangle that spans the entire floor.

"Can I ask you a quick question?" Lena asks a passing reporter. He raises his hands in the air, palms out, and keeps walking.

A harried woman passes. "Quick question—"

Lena feels like the child lost in the forest, only she can't remember which fairy tale. A dumpy man with a pen behind each ear approaches and she steps in his path.

"Boris Hackney's desk?"

Caligula Had It, Too

The man pivots and points toward a trio of men. Boris leans against a cubicle partition, his left leg slightly raised behind him, and dangles a narrow loafer from his foot. Another metro editor stands beside him, a man with red-rimmed eyes who seems to have no shoulders; his arms stick out from his torso, and he resembles nothing so much as a red-spotted newt. A wiry young reporter wears the look of privileged protest.

Their argument, like so many writer-editor struggles, recalls the British and the French discussing the Battle of Dunkirk: You let me down. No, *you* let *me* down.

"I don't have time to go back," the reporter says. "Can't we tweak it?"

"No, we can't *tweak* it," the newt says. "This is the *Record*. We don't tweak. You've got a story full of quotes from a Long Island construction worker who was on NPR yesterday bragging that he goes to news scenes so he can feed reporters quotes and see his name in the paper."

"Well," the reporter says, "he was a man on the street, technically speaking."

"He's a professional man on the street."

"They're good quotes."

"He's been quoted in the *Record* thirty-three times this year, Jim. His name has been in the *Record* more than yours has. Rewrite this now or I'll give him the byline and you can be the man on the street."

"The 'man on the street' quotes are all the same anyway. Everybody knows what people are going to say. If it's a serial killer, people say, He seemed like such a nice guy, kind of quiet, kept to himself. If it's—"

"Jim, nine thirty deadline. Do it. Dump it. Forget it."

"But there's a blackout. How am I—"

The newt shrugs and responds with what has become his famous non sequitur. "Dante had epilepsy, and Molière and Dickens. Tolstoy! Dostoyevsky and Moses and"— his voice rises with triumphant finality—"Caligula." He pads away in his socks toward the food table.

"Caligula?"

"That's a new one," Boris says.

Jim groans. "Why does he do that?"

Boris grins. "Hard to complain about rewriting nine hundred words when Dostoyevsky wrote *Crime and Punishment* with epilepsy."

"He probably didn't have an editor," Jim says glumly.

Lena tries to make eye contact with Boris, but he is studying the M&M's on his desk. So he's the one she's heard about. He asks clerks to line them up by color and to discard the red ones. She can't remember whether he hates the red ones or is afraid of them, and she wonders briefly where all the red ones go.

"Excuse me." Boris does not acknowledge her but gazes around the room and jiggles the loafer from his toes.

In the Battle of Dunkirk, she is Belgium.

Jim sits bent in his chair, head in hands. "Coleridge," he mutters, then louder, "Kafka." The newt pauses behind his cubicle and Jim turns to him. "Conrad!" he shouts. "Flau-Flaubert!"

The newt trembles slightly. "Epilepsy?" he whispers.

"Writer's block!" Jim shouts. "Creative inhibition. Writer's fucking block!"

"Now, now," the newt says, coming to stand over his desk. "All your notes, Casaubon," he says, slapping his cheek in mock distress. "All those rows of volumes—will you not make up your mind what part of them you will use, and begin to make your vast knowledge useful to the world?"

"Stop!" Jim shouts. "Stop quoting from nineteenth-century novels. I can't take it anymore. Why don't you teach high school?"

"Because this is more challenging, Jim."

Flooding the Zone

Boris hops up on the nearest desk, shoeless, and claps his hands twice. "Flood the zone, folks! We have to flood the zone! Why are you all standing around?" Clap, clap. "You all have your boroughs, now get to it. Let's see some enthusiasm!"

Lena stands with several reporters, gazing up at him. He hops from desk to desk, as if Vesuvius is erupting and he has found the one elevated area, which he intends to keep for himself.

"Metabolism!" he cries. "Let's see some high, high metabolism!"

"How many M&M's has he had?" one reporter mutters.

"You've got your assignments, people," Boris calls down to them. "Your chariot-carpools await downstairs."

The reporters scatter. Lena looks up at Boris and clears her throat. "Excuse me. I'm Lena from the Recording Room." She feels a dark blush flood her chest. "I'm here to—"

Boris looks down and cups his ear. "I can't hear you.

Here," he says, pushing a pink message pad with his foot, which is skinny and curved like a scythe. "Write it down."

She writes it down. It occurs to her that the doomed Vesuvians did try to bite the ankle of the elevated one. She considers the bony, silky-socked ankle.

Boris bends and reads from the pad at his feet: "My name is Lena. I am here from the Recording Room to take dictation."

The foot pushes a headset toward her. Boris points ("over there"), claps again, and hops away. A frantic news clerk shouts for someone to take a feed. Lena raises her headset in the air, and the clerk points to an empty cubicle.

Stories pour in as reporters call in from the five boroughs, creating their articles without pens or computers and passing their cell phones for direct quotes. Nurses in Bellevue are keeping premature babies alive in the dark after the generator overheats and quits. Stranded commuters wander onto the sidewalks as bars and restaurants fling open their doors to give away beer and ice cream.

"We're all sweaty, we're all hot, but so what? It's not terrorism. We're all alive and we might as well drink them while they're cold," says Ryan Bryan, a trader from Hoboken.

Lena takes call after call. On the Lower East Side a guy is serving beer to people sitting in traffic. In Bushwick, the neighborhood is quiet this time, unlike during the 1977 blackout. A forty-nine-year-old postal worker remembers the summer of '77 fondly because he acquired four couches, two or three stereos, and other "stuff." "Even the churchgoing folks were looting in seventy-seven," he says.

A Brooklyn-bound train is stuck on the Manhattan Bridge, and passengers can be seen "with their sweaty palms pressed against the windows."

Record of the Times

Across the room, a group has formed around Jim, who is muttering and banging his hands on the keyboard.

"Don't you have it yet, Jim?" Boris asks. "Just slug it, type it, dump it. We need it."

"It won't come," Jim says. "I'm blocked."

"What seems to be the trouble?" the newt asks before biting into a recently arrived barbecue sandwich from the buffet table.

"You're blocked?" Boris says. "What do you need, Ex-Lax?"

"Is that what you want me to produce?" Jim cries, looking up from his white computer screen. "Shit?"

"Come on, Jim," the newt says, "you're at the *Record*. You have every resource at your disposal."

"Yeah," says Boris, "so dispose."

"I can't write with you hovering."

"I know what you can write. Dear Miss Lonelyhearts, I'm a reporter who can't write. I work for the best newspaper in the world. Everyone takes my calls. When we have to work late, they feed us. I have an expense account that is never questioned. We have union hours and union compensation that allows us all to buy nice little houses in Montclair, where we're invited to dinner parties and tasteful social-justice demonstrations at the Unitarian church. But Miss Lonelyhearts, deadlines have got me down. Would it really be so bad if they gave my byline and a nice blank box where the words should be? Everyone knows my style anyhow."

"Oh, come off it, Boris. Go away."

Boris leans over and lowers his voice and hisses, "You may be one of Ralph's favorites," he says, "but you still have to meet deadlines."

Jim lifts his head and smiles at something past Boris's shoulder. "Yes, of course, I'll have it for you, Boris."

Boris turns, then—

The Man Who Loves Yeats

Everyone in the newsroom turns to silently acknowledge a man wearing a straw panama hat: the executive editor. Ralph passes by cubicles as if on a pulley, only his torso and head visible above the partitions. He ascends the staircase to heaven, and Lena remembers the memo he issued after the terrorist attacks, quoting Yeats: "a terrible beauty is born."

Just like a southerner, she says to herself, to give you Yeats when you need Celan.

There was earth inside them, and
they dug.

"Lord of the Flies," one of the reporters mutters. "No," another says. "Ralph was the hero. Jack was the leader, savage, self-absorbed bastard. Our Ralph is a Jack."

Lena has known that Ralph plays favorites and has sensed that he is losing popularity in the newsroom, but she hadn't known he is despised.

Another reporter joins the two and asks what they're talking about.

"Ralph."

"Did you see his article in *New York* magazine? Everything the man writes is a ten-thousand-word ode to himself."

"Yeah, even when it's two thousand."

LENA TAKES A call about the sewage disaster at the North River Wastewater Treatment Plant in Harlem, which is operating on generators, but millions of gallons of raw sewage have begun to collect and overflow.

A diver is preparing to swim through forty feet of black muck to find the faulty valve.

By 2 a.m., calls have dropped off and she removes her headset. She stands to go and looks around for permission to leave. Boris is nowhere to be seen, though she does spot his empty loafers on the food table. Someone has made celery-stick figures with baby carrot arms; the loafers are their boat. "Help" is spelled out in red M&M's.

She turns to look back at the newsroom from the stairwell door. Perhaps the rectangular room with the central spiral staircase is the right layout, because the news is laid out in columns, but in the center of all the stories are echoes of the past, the spiral of history.

Russell, with a red backpack slung over one shoulder, emerges from a cubicle and walks toward her.

"Hey, I hear they've set up a bar in the auditorium. Come check it out with me."

The back of the auditorium is dim, but generators are powering the lights onstage, where a long foldout table displays several liquor bottles and two Styrofoam coolers. A guy who looks too young to be an intern but is, in fact, a star business reporter is draped over one of the coolers. "It's melting the Styrofoam," he cries. "It's eating it! That's in my stomach." Several others gather around the cooler, scoop the pink liquid into paper cups, and cheer.

Russell grabs two beers and they find seats in the back row just as a suspiciously tan man enters the auditorium and strides toward the stage.

"Frank Slape," Russell says. "He used to be a good reporter, a very good reporter. He got his start in metro, made his name in Vietnam, became London bureau chief. And then he went all terrorism expert. Now he gabs and gabs all day, jabber, jabber, jabber, CNN, MSNBC, he'll talk to anybody with a camera and a big mike. Look at that face. It was a decent face and now he's just another talking head with orange makeup." He shakes his head sadly. "That's the walking demise of journalism right there. God, it was a sad day when the legs became the heads."

There is a cry from the stage, where Boris and some others have again snatched the memoir from the clerk's bag and take turns reading from it, standing on chairs and holding it up high as the clerk flails his arms uselessly in the air.

"I had crept under the covers of my parents' bed and had lain with them for several minutes before I rubbed my eyes and saw that there were four of us, not three. Mr. Jackson from across the street, the man with mutton-chops and the pretty wife whose hands often shook, was with us."

The reporters answer with catcalls. Many expressions pass across the clerk's face—humiliation, anger, streaks of frustration. A twitching smile also tugs at the corners of his mouth because this is the most attention his writing has ever received from the *Record*.

"It's nice to see you out of the Recording Room," Russell says. "I don't think I've ever seen you anywhere else, except locked away with your machine. Not in the hall, not in the elevator, even — "

"Do you think I'm a ghost?"

"No, of course not. It's just nice to see you out, that's all. But you look sad."

"The job is starting to wear on me. It's hard sitting in that room all day with the tapes and the headsets. Does the news ever get to you?"

"I'm a reporter. We're all junkies. So there's no hope for us."

"I sit alone all day with the voices. I'm turning into a tape recorder," she says. "It's frightening. I'm turning into a machine."

He leans in and kisses her lightly along the hairline, near her ear. "No, not a machine at all."

"Thanks," she says, averting her face with shy pleasure. "Do you know what caused the blackout?"

"Not yet. Some are blaming Canada, some are blaming Ohio. Some are blaming birds."

"Birds?"

"It's the least likely theory, seems nearly impossible on this scale. But they found a pile of dead pigeons under a huge power line. So someone came up with the brilliant theory that they all perched up there together and flapped their wings in unison and committed mass suicide, causing a short in the line that caused a kind of chain reaction."

"Pigeon mass suicide?"

"Well, you know, they make good scapegoats."

"Like Canada?"

He smiles and she notices that he looks tired. It is the first time she has seen him unshaven. So, he grows actual stubble like other men.

"Is it possible?"

"Is what possible?"

"About the pigeons."

"Barely. It was probably something simple—trees weren't trimmed, power lines went out, electricity found other routes and caused power surges. From there, relays shut down parts of the grid, and then, a cascade of failures."

" 'Cascade of failures,' nice phrase."

"Thanks. We were halfway through a case of warm Rolling Rock when the prose began to flow. I think that's the same time the bird blackout theory developed."

"Drinking in the newsroom?"

"A little. Are you shocked?"

"No, relieved."

"Well, it's not the Gray Lady."

She sees that he has a cowlick and just below, on his forehead, the faint imprint of four print-stained fingers.

"You have a" —she motions to his face— "newsprint tattoo."

He rubs his forehead and blushes. "The dangers and indignities of journalism."

He leans toward her, takes off his glasses, and is more exposed than if he were naked. His eyes are weak, vulnerable, expectant. Journalists terrify her with their endless need.

"Carol, are you OK?"

"I have to go, Russell. I have to go."

The air on the street is just as stifling and still as it was inside the building, and Times Square is a concrete cage. She walks along with others as if wading through wet black wool, following the illuminated path just beyond her flashlight. People are still out, but now they all seem sleepy drunk and disoriented from gulping warm beer and black air.

At Parkside her room is sweltering, and she opens the window wide, slumps down in a chair, and rests her head on the sill. The city has changed into a strange and silent place, as if blanketed in black snow. She can hear the distant sound of drunken voices from the unseen streets. She stares outside, remembering the brick wall opposite and the snatch of Gramercy Park that can be seen to the left. If white is the color of panic, what is blackness, this blackness? A black blanket thrown over the panic, not snuffing it out, no, not the absence of panic, not here, not now, not anymore. But still it is a soothing darkness, a hot black frost that, for once, allows New Yorkers to spill out onto the streets with a sense of wonder that they can never show in the light. And more thrilling is the notion that there is danger underneath, that they are children walking on the sleeping dragon's back.

She reaches behind her without turning, touches the telephone. The plastic receiver feels solid in her sweaty hands. She lifts it, still not turning, and lets it drop. She repeats the movement and listens to the sound of the receiver dropping back into its cradle. The third time, she turns toward the phone, groping for it in the darkness. She lifts the receiver, hears the dial tone, punches the Recording Room number by touch. The overnight machine clicks and she hears her own voice.

"You have reached the Recording Room's dictation mailbox. Please note that this voice mailbox has a maximum duration of twenty minutes. If your dictation is longer than twenty minutes and you are disconnected, please hang up and call back to continue dictating. Your copy will be transcribed during working hours, which start at nine a.m. Please begin with your name, location, and the desk or editor who should receive the transcript. Please include punctuation for accuracy, speak at a normal conversational pace, and spell names phonetically, the first time only. Begin dictating when you hear the tone."

She hears the ancient tone and sits in the dark holding the receiver.

"Note to self," she says, as she usually does when she calls to leave herself a reminder for the morning. But tonight she can't think of anything to say. "Note to self," she repeats. She hangs up, but after a few minutes, she dials again. "You have reached the Recording Room . . ."

"Hello," she says, "this is Lena." She is surprised at herself, at her own voice, and she waits in the silence.

"I guess this is crazy. Of course you can't hear me. I mean, not like that. Right? But I saw you on the bus and I really want to talk to you. I can't say why, exactly, but it's true.

"How to begin? It's dark here, too, tonight. There's been a blackout, and the whole city is a blind spot except the small seeing-spots made by flashlights.

"They say the blind have heightened other senses to compensate. Did you feel you had to listen to everything? Didn't you ever get tired of listening? I do.

"What did you see when you lived in darkness? We are all looking into the darkness here, longing to see what is no longer there."

She hangs up and lays her head on the windowsill. A sudden summer rain is coming, the air smells of it, and a damp breeze comes through the window. Looking into the blacked-out night, she thinks of all the solitary places she has hidden from the mountain lion, and though she has never found him, he has always tracked her. She wonders why an imaginary beast has always come for her, and she stares into the darkness trying to face the terror of the unseen.

CHAPTER FOUR

City Loses Body of Woman Killed by Lions; Blackout Blamed on Canada

In the morning, she awakens in the chair, rubs her stiff neck, and flips the light switch. Power.

She buys the *Record* on her way to work and sits on a bench to scan the headlines. Katheryn's Baghdad bombing article is on page 7. She scans it almost without reading, like a seamstress scanning a garment for a loose stitch. She scans the article a second time and a third before she realizes what she is searching for. The charred foot is gone, edited out. First, it is ripped from the body. Then even the phantom foot is amputated from the black skeleton of newspaper ink.

She lives in this shadow state, always reading the news

she knows over the news that makes it into print, and not just reading the shadows, but also living in them, somewhere between waiting and searching. This is what chills her, the erasure, the amputation, the phantom words. Sometimes these lost words that have been edited out of existence drift through her dreams in the form of a monster dropping unmatched shoes and lifeless limbs, charred feet, so that in her nightmare she must chase after the floating creature, holding up these nameless, possessionless things, crying, "You dropped something. Don't you need this? Don't you?"

IN THE RECORD'S lobby, she nods to the security guards, swipes her photo ID (they're fatter now: the new ones have microchips, making it easier to identify bodies in the rubble).

In the elevator, she stares at her shoes because it seems unfair to see fellow Recordians so close up. It is undeniable whose hair is thinning, who wears too much cologne, who should wear a little more. Sometimes she recognizes reporters whose interviews she has transcribed. There are a few of them who speak to her, but most of them don't. Standing so close, she remembers personal things they have probably forgotten that they revealed. It used to surprise her how much the reporters talk about themselves. The business reporter on her left is on Atkins; married six months, he hunted the "big five" on his honeymoon safari in Kenya. Legrande Haze, the flak-jacket-wearing metro reporter who gets on at the third floor, once bit a member of the housekeeping staff.

The doors open and she automatically glances up. Breath is sucked in. People move quickly, bumping into one another. She is pinned against the back panel, a broad-shouldered block of a man before her: advertising manager, wears his class ring and ties with tiny golf clubs. She cannot see, but then she hears. It is the publisher. Someone speaks to him, calls him by name, Howard—that's what everyone calls him to his face. Sometimes behind his back they use his nickname, Kernel, which he is said to hate, just as his father hated his—Popcorn. Or maybe he didn't. She has never seen Popcorn, doesn't know if he's still living. He retired in the 1990s, before she came to the *Record,* and is spoken of with reverence, with words like "dignity," "constancy," "legacy." But perhaps that is because he presided over the *Record* during its golden years.

Someone asks Howard about his father. The query is perfectly scripted, just like Lena learned in a mandatory development workshop. You are always to have two thirty-second dialogues prepared (one social, one professional) in case you are in the elevator with "senior management."

The publisher wears critter suspenders and is said to be a sort of nice man.

She pushes the Recording Room door open—the handle is still waiting for the repair team—hangs the phones on their hooks, checks the overnight machine. The gray machine (the dimensions of a 1950s bread box) shows one recorded call, her own. She presses "erase." "Are you sure you want to erase?" the screen prompts. "If yes, press 'erase' now." She pauses, then presses "save."

The pigeon jumps as usual when she raises the blinds.

"Alarmed anew," she says, tapping on the glass. "And yet every day it's the same." She lifts the window. "I said, every day it's the same. How's life on the ledge?"

But the bird shows no interest.

"You know, pigeon, when you stand on the ledge, eventually you have to jump off. That's kind of the point."

The pigeon remains unmoved by this observation.

"Where did you come from?" She leans out and looks left and right. "Aren't pigeons supposed to mate for life? Who ever heard of a bachelor pigeon? And I know you're a male. I see it in your indifferent eyeballs. Were you a homing pigeon who got tired? Or did you just abandon your flock? Tired of the wife and kids, of being pigeon-pecked and holding the family together with string and seed and recycled straw? Well, if you came looking for anonymity, you came to the right ledge."

She backs away from the window, leaving it partly open. Today's *Record:* The Catholic Church has removed babies from limbo. A Mount Everest climber is left to die as his fellow trekkers file past him. The Colombian Nukak tribe has decided to join modern civilization. They walked naked out of the forest and are living in an encampment just inside the city. They have no concept of property, government, countries, money, or words like "future." When asked if they are sad, they say no and "howl with laughter."

Her hand, which has been holding the corner of the page, drops. It is not Russell's byline; it is a wire story about the blind woman.

"Arlene Lebow, who committed suicide by entering the lions' den at the Bronx Zoo, is missing. Ms. Lebow's sister, Ellen Lebow, who did not learn of her sister's death until yesterday, has been trying to locate the body.

"A spokesman for Mount Sinai, Fred Klamm, confirmed that Ms. Lebow was admitted on July 8. After death was declared, her body was sent to the hospital morgue and then to the city morgue at Bellevue Hospital Center.

" 'We take this very seriously,' Mr. Klamm said. 'We try very hard to find relatives of the deceased.'

"The morgue was not able to locate Ms. Lebow's name in its records, but the director of public affairs said officials were continuing to check.

"Ellen Lebow said she learned of her sister's death

when she got a call from the hospital's billing department concerning the ambulance that transported Ms. Lebow from the zoo to the hospital.

"It is possible that Ms. Lebow was buried in the city's potter's field on Hart Island, but no burial record has been found.

" 'They say I owe them $595,' Ellen Lebow said, referring to an ambulance bill from Mount Sinai. 'But they owe me my sister.' "

LENA CLOSES THE paper and snaps the interview tape into the Dictaphone, but she can't concentrate, can't empty out to accept the words.

She can see the article on Arlene from her chair; the newspaper lies open on her desk. Arlene is a fragile skeleton of black ink on a bed of cheap pulp paper. To-morrow she will be yesterday's news, her body blowing along the gutter, perhaps stepped or spit on, dropped in the street, and embedded in a tire's tread as the car continues on, its unknowing occupants cursing or singing or laughing.

She takes a scarf from her bag and spreads it over the desk, folding it slowly, carefully, and tying it over her eyes, snug, then looser, then snug again. The keyboard feels smooth and foreign under her fingers and she pulls the scarf down to see whether she has typed anything by accident. She has not. She readjusts the scarf and presses the foot pedal. The soundless time on the tape begins, and she listens, concentrating for the first word in the dark.

In the waiting, she realizes it is not a mask she has been searching for but a hood, with no opening for eyes, mouth, nose. Just darkness.

"At the end of the day," the business reporter is saying, "this shopping mall is—"

"No, no, no," another voice says. It's the owner of a new skyscraper near Central Park. "Please do not call it a shopping mall. It is not a shopping mall. It is a vertical luxury experience."

How can a body with a name disappear along with all the edited words? Lena wonders while typing. If Arlene has been buried in a potter's field, it will be as if she never existed.

"I see," says the reporter. "Then in this vertical experience—"

"It's not just any skyscraper," the skyscraper owner says. "We have worked very hard to preserve the views of Central Park with a European glass curtain wall. Each of my properties has its own intellectual soul. That's why in Harlem we are building a residential property that evokes a giraffe."

"You're talking about the boutique hotel chain that is in the West Village, Chelsea, the Lower East Side, and—"

"No, no, no," the voice says. "We are not a chain. We are a small luxury hotel experience. We have a pillow concierge at every luxury location. We have butlers who were trained by the former butler for the Prince of Wales."

She closes her eyes behind the scarf and types with the automatic hearing she has developed over the past four years. It is as if her hearing has two levels. On the automatic level, she hears the words that stream through the headphones, fading in and out: "the view is free . . . all are welcome . . ." And on the second level, she hears what she recites to herself while transcribing, often poetry. She blinks, pushes the scarf up on her forehead, lifts her foot off the pedal, and looks at what she has typed: "The vertical luxury experience is *pull down thy vanity, I say pull down.* For example, the stunning view of Central Park is free to *all in the not done, all in the diffidence that faltered.*"

"I suppose they wouldn't want Ezra Pound in the vertical luxury experience," she says aloud, as she backs the cursor across the screen and watches the letters disappear. This is a danger of the job. When she is in her transcriptionist's trance, she types whatever rolls through her head. This is why she once had a film director appreciating the "signage in porn films" instead of "the signage in foreign films."

She presses the foot pedal, lifts it again. She pulls the scarf back down around her eyes and types. For long stretches it seems that she has eliminated the need to hear and is simply the conduit, transferring the voice from tape to type. The tape turns around its spool, and the voices go on and on; the sound comes through her earbuds, as if it has to travel no distance at all, as if the voices originate in her ear and bloom there.

The interviewee asks to go off the record. It surprises Lena that when people ask to go off the record, the reporter always agrees yet very rarely turns off the tape recorder. At first she did not know whether she should transcribe off-the-record comments. She felt guilty listening to them, but nothing has ever been revealed that she found shocking. So now she transcribes the off-the-record words with all the others, and she does not even pause when she types the stage direction in brackets for the transcript: "[Interviewee requests to go off the record for the following comments.]"

The tape ends, the voices stop, and she removes her headset, unties the scarf. Standing at the window, she looks at the pigeon. "Free among us. Is that why people hate you? No smashing success, no shattering failure, nothing to prove, no fear of being sent back to Ohio or Kansas or Iowa. You're simply adaptable, indestructible."

Suddenly self-conscious, she turns from the window, takes the phones off the hooks to forward calls to the overnight machine, and walks out without closing the door. She takes the stairs to the vending machines on the fifth floor. The floor is shiny gray, the hallway is wider than on other floors, and large drums of what Lena has always assumed are printing chemicals line the wall. She passes a long file cabinet with drawers labeled A to Y (no Z) and a red sign that says NO LOITERING. No loitering? The floor is completely deserted.

She pauses at each of the four vending machines to study the selections of chips, candy bars, crackers, peanuts, which brings to mind the schoolyard stories of biting into peanut candy bars so old they are full of worms.

The fluorescent lights buzz overhead, almost covering another fainter, human sound. She looks in both directions: no one. There is a room across the hall, but the blue double doors are closed and she hears no movement behind them.

She turns back to the limited offerings and wonders how often they fill these machines. There's Shasta cream soda, A&W root beer, Vernors ginger ale, and Mightee grape soda, cans so old they could be colored tin reliquaries.

She gives the machines a final look and turns to leave, empty handed. There it is again, the sound. She stands still and listens. A cough. Yes, definitely a cough. She crosses the hall and puts her ear to the blue door. Another cough, and then the muffled sound of a man's voice singing: "Now the day is over—damn, now how did it go?" A sigh.

She lifts her head and looks at the closed door. Who could this be? The man who fills the vending machines got locked in a room twenty years ago and never escaped?

Automatically, her right hand rises to her shoulder, ready to rap on the door. She looks at her fist and lets it drop.

"Now the day is over," the thin voice repeats, trailing off.

Definitely an old man. She could transcribe this voice, could identify it from a panel of voices. She knocks lightly.

No answer.

She clears her throat. "Sir? I think it's 'Night is drawing nigh,'" she half sings to the closed door.

"That's it," the voice says. "Of course, 'Night is drawing nigh.'"

There is a pause and she takes two steps back and waits.

"Shadows of the evening—" Pause. "Shadows of the evening—"

She realizes she is being prompted, so she sing-says, "Um, steal across the sky."

There are shuffling sounds.

"Who's there?"

"Lena."

The door opens a few inches and a lined face appears in the gap, as if suspended. "Who sent you?"

"No one, no one, I just—I was at the vending machines"—she turns and points—"and I heard you. I'm sorry, I didn't mean to interrupt. I heard your voice and was curious."

The door opens a few more inches.

"Did anyone see you?"

"No."

He motions her inside. The room is a large square that gets its light from a row of north-facing windows, some of which have been patched neatly with newspaper and masking tape. Tall metal shelves filled with ancient-looking volumes line one wall. One of the clothbound volumes, a bottle of clear liquid, and a cloth are on a round table in the center of the room, along with a few browning bananas. The scent of ripe fruit mixes with the smell of old paper, the sweet smell of decay.

"You can keep a secret, can't you?"

"Yes."

She waits for the secret to be revealed, but he seems satisfied with the silence and follows her gaze to the bananas on the table. There is one deep crease across his wide forehead, like a bird's wingspan drawn by a child.

"Is this your work?" she asks, nodding at the open volume.

"I'm trying to mend these obituaries," he says. "Until I patched the holes in the windows, this had become a pigeon coop. And you know the way of the living, they are not always attentive to the dead."

"So you're a preservationist."

A sharp knock sounds at the window and he crosses the room silently and lifts the window by the painted-over iron handles. A pigeon peers in from the ledge.

"This is a bold one. He always wants to dine alone." He opens a brown paper bag and sprinkles crumbs on the sill. "He always returns after the others have gone."

While the man is busy at the window, she looks around. Hulking green file cabinets take up the middle of the room. There is a neat pallet in the corner. He can't live here, and yet it seems that he might.

"Do you like pigeons?" he asks, closing the window and coming to sit at the table.

"I never really thought about it." Befriending pigeons does seem frighteningly eccentric—at least it used to seem that way—but she can't say that, especially since she's begun talking to them herself. There is a man she sees sometimes in the park who sits very still until pigeons perch on him, his shoulders, his legs, his head. He feeds them and occasionally announces, "I'm a monument."

"They're tenacious, I suppose."

He nods.

"Maybe invincible. Darwin liked pigeons, right? All

pigeons descend from one pigeon? Still, they certainly do, you know—"

"Shit a lot?"

"Yes."

"It's the older volumes that were exposed to their droppings," he says, pointing to the shelf along the wall. "Those"—he points to the file cabinets—"are safe in their mass industrial tomb."

"All those are obits, too?"

He nods. "It's bulky, but not as big as you'd think for all those bodies."

"How many are in there?"

"Thousands. They're full, been full for a long time. That's why no one comes in here. There's no space left in the morgue, and anyway, they use computers now. All that waiting upstairs, being researched, being written, being edited." He snaps his fingers. "And then in the space of a day, printed, recycled."

"In the space of a day," she agrees. "So all those stories are just forgotten. All those people, the disappeared."

"It's important to remember," he says, "but it's important to make room, too. That's what my son says anyway."

She has heard about the *Record*'s morgue, the vast collection of clips with a legendary card catalog of news makers and bios of those whose obits wait to be written or, in some cases, are written and wait only to be updated and printed. Some of the obits have been written years in advance, the occasional result being a *Record* obituary with the byline of a deceased writer.

"Don't people come in here sometimes to get clips?"

He shakes his head. "The morgue, this morgue anyway, has been forgotten. It's all been digitized. It's hard to believe, but that's what they say. Those in the filing cabinets are just the paper copies. The digital files and the microfiche have been moved to a building on Sixth Avenue. They don't call it the morgue anymore. They call it the archive. The morgue has ceased to exist."

He looks at her, his hazel eyes uncomfortably observant, the curtain of his pupils parted, as if she could enter purgatory through his eyes.

She takes the newspaper clipping of Arlene from her pocket and smooths it out on the table. He does not comment but continues to look at her; his face is abraded, as if it has been painted, scraped away, repainted, scraped away, worked and worn, remnants of the past still visible.

"Who's this?"

"She's been lost, too, in a different kind of morgue."

"She's dead though."

"Yes."

"Some of my best friends are dead."

"I saw her the day she died, or the day before, a matter of days at most. We were on the same bus. We talked a little, it seemed a bit strange but not distressingly so. And now she's dead. She killed herself in the lions' den, or had the lions do it. And I can't help thinking now, what if she was asking me something and I wasn't listening? It—she haunts me."

"We haunt ourselves." He holds out his hand, which she shakes, surprised at his grip. "My name is Kov."

"I'm Lena."

"Lena," he says, looking down at the article, "it looks like there's enough information here to start your search."

"But she's dead, and her body's been lost."

"She has a sister."

"Contact her sister? That would be presumptuous, an imposition."

"Well, then, there's only the lion."

"I doubt he's talking."

"Depends on what you're asking."

CHAPTER FIVE

Mudslide Buries Hundreds in Pakistan; Teenagers Say Oral Sex Is Not Sex

In the hall she turns back and looks at the closed blue door, which she never knew opened onto the forgotten files of the dead. The *Record* records, but it doesn't remember. Neither does she. Already she is uncertain of Arlene's face, the sharpness of her features, the length of her fingers. She does not take the elevator to the eleventh floor; she takes the stairs, two at a time, up six flights.

In the Recording Room she picks up the phone and dials information. She cannot give herself time to look in the phonebook. She cannot give herself time to think, time to change her mind. The automated voice gives her the number for Bellevue and she dials quickly with shaking hands.

"Hello," she says into the receiver. "I'm calling for information about Arlene Lebow."

"Who are you?"

"I'm Lena Respass," she says. "I'm a reporter for the *Record*."

"What's your press number?"

"My press number?"

"Yes, your press number. Anybody could call and say they were a reporter for the *Record*. What did you say your name was again?"

"My name . . . ," she says weakly before hanging up.

She looks out the dirty window at the cheap hotel across the street. The pigeon stares without moving when she leans out beside him.

"I'm not going to panic, pigeon. People probably lie to get information all the time. Anyway, she won't remember my name."

They both look at the strip of black pavement below and then west, toward the Hudson. She leans farther over the extended window ledge, which is like a small cement balcony, rectangular and thigh-deep. I don't know what it's called, she thinks. I don't know the word for it. There is a slight breeze; it's quiet and peaceful above the city. Seen from above, taxis seem to glide instead of jerk; tourists look serene and bovine in their slow-moving herds.

"New York, give me some of you! New York come to me the way I came to you, my feet over your streets, you pretty town I loved you so much." She brushes off her hands and pulls her head back inside. "Pigeon," she says, tapping the window, "those are the words of Mr. Arturo Bandini, though he was talking about LA. We probably wouldn't do too well in LA, you and me. You have to drive. That's right, if you won't fly you'll have to drive to the gym to ride the exercise bike."

Someone coughs behind her and she turns to see Russell studying her with his head tilted to the side. For several long seconds, neither of them utters a word. She turns back to the window. This would be a good time to jump.

"Hi, Carol."

"Hi, Russell."

She waits for him to laugh or make a joke about her talking to pigeons, but he doesn't. He doesn't, but he does look behind her, at the window.

"Russell, do you ever track people down? I mean, do you ever wonder about the people you write about, what their lives are like after you write about them, about their lives off the page?"

"No, not really, it would drive a reporter mad."

"Well, if you were tracking someone down for a story, if you were looking for someone, how would you go about it?"

"Are they lost?"

"I don't know."

"Well, you could try the Internet, or, the old-fashioned way, look in the white pages."

"Right, it's just that . . ."

He lets go of the door and looks at her directly, which he seldom does. Usually he is looking down at the tape in his hands or at the window blinds. "It's just what, Carol?"

"It's difficult to explain."

"Well, it's more difficult if they don't want to be found. Do they want to be found?"

"I'm not sure."

"Well, you start with a name. Everyone has a name."

"Yes," she says. "Some of us have more than one."

And with timing that makes her suspect that the gods are both bored and malicious, Morris the art critic sticks his head in the door.

"Lena, how busy are you?"

Morris is the other Recordian who calls her by name.

"Her name—" Russell starts to say, but she cuts him off.

"Hi, Morris. I need to finish something for Russell first. Do you know each other?"

They shake hands, say they know of each other.

"What do you have, Morris? And when do you need it?"

"This is an interview with the artist Veronica Vax. Do you know her work?"

Lena and Russell nod politely. Veronica Vax's exhibits involve a group of naked women with model measurements standing still for hours while wearing dominatrix stilettos and singing nursery rhymes. In Paris they wore blindfolds designed by Karl Lagerfeld. In New York, Chanel key chains dangled from their pubic hair, which was groomed into logos by the photographer Terry Richardson.

"I think it's quite fascinating how she reifies post-modern hegemony—"

"Please stop." Lena closes her eyes and leans against the panel of telephones.

"Are you all right?" Russell asks, putting a hand on her arm. "You look pale."

"It's nothing."

"Just do the best you can with this," Morris says.

"Sure, you're second in line."

She picks up the request form and sees—on the line asking the date the transcript is needed—he has written "ASAP," just above the plea to "please be more specific than ASAP."

"I'll get to it as soon as possible," she says, and Morris strolls out.

"You went white just now," Russell says. "Are you sure you're all right?"

"Yes. It just reminded me of graduate school. Whenever I hear about reifying the hegemony, I want to run for my life."

"What was the program?"

"Literature."

"Why'd you quit?"

"I was cured." She does not say what she really feels about language failing her, because it is too painful to think of the time when she believed that language could save people.

"How were you cured?"

"With time, I guess. Academic language is wretched. And after reading works like 'Reclaiming the Clit: Lacan and the Metastasis of Masturbation,' or 'A Womb of His Own: Male Renaissance Poets in the Female Body,' I thought—"

"All the best titles were taken?"

"Something like that."

She almost says, but doesn't, that it would have meant renouncing the language of her origins, the language of the rural South. That she could not do this had surprised her most of all. She had had no trouble renouncing all the rest of it—the church, the landscape, even her own family. She had not visited her father in two years when he died from a snakebite. Apparently he had poured hydrogen peroxide on the wound and went about weeding the ditch until he sat down and died, a bloodstained rag around the hand that still held the hoe when he was found the following day.

"Was it really that bad?" Russell asks.

"There was also 'Autoerotics, Anal Erotics, and'—"

"Stop, stop! Consider my sensitive journalist's ears."

He covers his ears, then uncovers them when she purses her lips together. "Carol, why didn't you correct Morris just now when he called you Lena? A little postgraduate vindictiveness, laughing at the critic behind his back?"

"Oh, it's not that important."

"It's your name, Carol, of course it's important."

"Oh, that."

"I was going to correct him, but I thought you would."

"Russell, it's just that"—she takes a deep breath and says it quickly, quietly, on the exhale—"my name is Lena."

He winces. "You mean all this time . . . and you never . . . and I—"

"I'm sorry. At first it didn't matter and then it was too late."

"I can't believe all this time you let me call you by the wrong name."

"I'm sorry, Russell." Maybe she has it all wrong. She hadn't been amused by his mistake, but still she hadn't corrected him. Maybe it is true that sins of omission are as bad as all the others.

The phone rings and she presses "record," lifts the receiver.

"Bye, Lena."

"I'm sorry, Russell," she says, but he is walking away and doesn't turn back. She steps out into the hall with the phone pressed to her ear and the long umbilical phone cord trailing behind her. She watches him step into the elevator and she backs into the Recording Room, wraps the cord around her fingers, pushes the door closed with her foot.

The call is from a foreign reporter, Eric Isaacs, who is having technical problems and is unable to send his story by e-mail. He is one of Lena's favorite journalists; there is modesty in his voice and he always recognizes her as a human on the other end of the line. He does not give punctuation, and in this case she takes it as a show of respect. Today he dictates five paragraphs about a mudslide in Pakistan that has left many dead or missing. Then the line goes dead.

" 'The earth shook, then I felt mud in my mouth.'

"The mud is thirty to forty feet deep in places, and authorities fear that some bodies will not be found."

Lena empties out and presses the foot pedal, letting the words flow through.

"But the search for four-year-old Aarya will go on, according to her uncle, who said they would continue digging until she was recovered.

" 'We will not leave anyone behind,' he said. 'That is not our way.' "

There was earth inside them, and
they dug.

They dug and dug, and so
their day went past, their night.

While she is transcribing, an envelope slides through the door's mail slot and falls on the floor. She ignores it and continues to type. Sometimes reporters don't enter the Recording Room; they just put their tapes in envelopes and drop them through the slot. She can e-mail the finished transcript, drop the tapes in interoffice mail, and eliminate any need for personal contact.

She is standing by the recording phones rewinding the tape when she looks down and sees that she is standing on the envelope. She picks it up; it is too light and flat to hold a tape. Inside is a single sheet of paper, a photocopy.

The paper is light as ash in her hands. She tilts it toward the light, and her hand trembles slightly. It is beautiful. In the X-rayed image, the bird is helpless and appears to be lying on his back. All he possesses, anonymous bones, laid bare. The bones do not look brittle, but solid where they should be solid and light where they should be light. The skull, which seems impossibly small, is the perfect size to cap the bean-size brain. How can bones be so white, the white of a thousand frosts, when they have never been exposed to any elements?

Here is the homely pigeon, transformed.

There is a soft knock on the door.

"Hi, Russell."

"Lena, I came back because I didn't want you to think I was mad. What's this?" he asks, putting his coffee cup down on the transcription log and picking up the X-ray.

"Someone dropped it through the mail slot."

"What, a joke? This is creepy. Do you know who did it?"

"No, it's not creepy. Yes, I know who."

"Are you sure it's a joke? It looks sinister to me."

She takes the paper from his hand. "It's a sort of calling card. I think it's beautiful," she says. "Look at how delicate, look at the wing bones."

"Beautiful?" He walks past her to the window, separates the blinds with his fingers, and looks out. "Like your friend out here on the ledge?"

She doesn't answer but picks up his coffee cup, which is smudged with ink fingerprints, and turns it in her hand.

"The journalist's signature. In another century, words were written on the fingertips to help meditation," she says. "Touching your fingers would help you remember." She lightly presses her nails. "Repent, confess, and be content."

Russell closes his eyes and touches his fingertips. "Rules of the road, ethics hotline, without fear or favor."

"Are you dropping off a tape?"

"What? No. I just—some of us are going for drinks after work. Would you like to go?"

"Oh, OK."

SHE SPENDS THE afternoon transcribing an interview for a Sunday magazine story about kids and oral sex. With her headphones on she lapses into her transcriptionist's trance; she is invisible and has perfect hearing. The voices fill her entire head, they are protected inside her skull, she gives herself up, lets the words course through, and lays them gently but quickly on the page. "Sex is a humongous thing," a fourteen-year-old girl says on the tape, "but oral sex isn't the same as sex."

As she leaves the *Record,* the magazine interview plays in her head. The girls had spoken without self-consciousness about giving blow jobs. She thinks how strange it is that the social code of girlhood has changed so much in a generation: reputation used to depend on the secrecy of certain acts, and now reputation depends on the publicizing of them.

The bar is a journalist hangout and she recognizes several *Record* reporters, but she doesn't see Russell. She orders a scotch and studies the rows of bottles lined up behind the bar in accordance with the universal bar-stocking chart. The universal poster taped to the wall by the cash register shows how to help a tubular figure demonstrating the universal choking sign.

As she sips her drink and looks in the mirror, gazing around the room, she sees Katheryn Keel. What is it about her that marks her so clearly as a predator? Lena wonders. It seems strange that one can see it straight-away, even from the back. She's nearly six feet, but it's not the height; it's something in the stance, or maybe it's in the faces of the crowd around her. They are like pets just after the terror of being tamed has left their eyes, and now they are docile, content, eager to please.

The man Katheryn is clutching as she holds court is Russell. He smiles at something she says and lifts his head to glance around the room. When their eyes meet, he breaks from Katheryn's grip and joins her.

"How are you?" His voice sounds different, though she couldn't say how. "Lena, it's nice to see you out of your cell."

Katheryn comes toward them. She is wearing a black silk jumpsuit and, on her huge flat feet, kitten-heel mules, which cause her to sway ever so slightly; overall, she gives the impression of a highly focused, structurally so-phisticated, and quite expensive effort, like a skyscraper reinforced against the wind effect.

"Katheryn is just back from Baghdad," Russell says as he introduces them.

"Russell says you work in the transcription room. It's so quaint, so obsolete. But I used it the other day when I was leaving Baghdad."

"I transcribed your story, it was about the bombing in the market."

Katheryn does not respond but looks up and makes contact with herself in the mirror above the bar, then scans the room for a new audience. Her eyes narrow and she leans against a barstool and kicks off her mules, one of which hits Zibby, a styles reporter, in the arm.

"Ow!"

"I just can't keep them on another minute. I've always thought women who insist on deforming their feet are idiots."

"That heel hurt. Glad you didn't take my eye out, Katheryn."

Katheryn rocks back and forth on the balls of her feet, and everyone is made conscious that she is the tallest woman in the bar. A group of reporters, sniffing a Katheryn war story, drift over.

"That's nothing. Have you ever been shot at?"

No, they all say, they have not.

"Well," she says, closing her eyes and inhaling through her nose, "there's nothing like it for feeling alive. There's something that happens in war zones, it's life at its best as well as life at its worst."

"Maybe it's best because it's—" Russell says, but she cuts him off with a wave of her hand.

"Nothing else can compare," she says, "to being embedded with the United States Marines. The smell of war." She does another eye-clench, nostril-flare.

Someone says, "The smell of—" but stops as Katheryn opens her eyes and stares with a hardness that stills them all.

"When I was with those men, the Seventh Marines, in the desert in our BDUs—"

"Our BDUs? You're a journalist—"

"What are BDUs?" Zibby asks.

"Battle dress uniforms."

"I thought journalists weren't supposed to wear military uniforms," Lena says.

Katheryn shrugs and winks. "I looked magnificent. Just kidding. It made sense at the time. When you're in the desert with the boys and you're the only journalist with access, it makes sense to wear the uniform. I was the objective observer." She makes her voice even louder. "I was the lens, no, the organ, the organ through which the moral view of the marines was made visible."

"But you're—"

"I said it made sense for me to wear it, Lena. Lena here is a transcriptionist, did you all know that? She types up our work. Isn't that wonderfully old fashioned? As I was saying, I was the first journalist to embed in Baghdad. And BDUs were a hell of a lot better than kitten heels, even in the heat of hell. But I was talking about the edge, the clarity, the exhilaration of walking in lockstep with death. After a long day in the desert, we drove through Fallujah and stopped at an open marketplace. It was a good day, blazing hot, and no one had died. Some children were playing outside the market and one of them tossed a ball to a marine."

The ceramic plate from her body armor is lying on the bar and she picks it up like a trophy and holds it awkwardly with both hands. Everyone is mesmerized by the oddity of it.

"It was just an automatic response, right? Someone throws something, especially a child, and you catch it. Except it wasn't a ball he threw to the marine. It was an IED." She tosses the plate in the air.

"Watch out!" Zibby shouts as Katheryn catches it at the last moment. "That's dangerous. You're dangerous."

"You should have seen the poor marine, nineteen years old and he had to be scraped up with the dirt. Poor kid was just playing catch with a child, trying to be friendly. The civilian instinct, that's what kills you."

"You mean he died?"

"Of course he died, Zibby. He caught an IED with his hands. What do you think?"

"I thought this was a story about being shot at," Lena says.

Katheryn plops the plate on the bar. "Aren't you a precise one? I think I made my point—"

"That the instinct to be a friendly, decent human being can kill you," one of the reporters says to laughter. "That explains why you and Ralph hit it off."

"Thank God for Ralph," Katheryn says. "For all his faults, and they are multitudinous, the man knows how to run a newsroom. He understands that news is not about nuance. You have to be bold, you have to overwhelm with the *Record*'s force and set the national agenda. Listen to me, Russell, I can help you, dear. I may not have Ralph by the balls anymore but I still have his ears, which, by the way, are much more satisfying."

"Katheryn!" Zibby says. "You are so vulgar. And such a braggart."

"You know you love it, Zibby. Besides, it ain't bragging if you really done it."

Lena is settling her bar tab when Russell reaches out to grab her arm, but he misses and rests his hand awkwardly on the back of her barstool. She watches him try to think of what to say.

"You look pensive."

"I was wondering—Eric Isaacs called in a lead about the mudslide in Pakistan but never called back with the adds. It's not like him. I wondered if you'd heard anything."

"Heard what?"

"It's just that he always calls back with his adds. Do you know if anyone has heard from him?"

"Eric knows how to take care of himself. You shouldn't worry. He probably just lost the phone line. And he's so busy; he's writing a book about American involvement in Pakistan."

She excuses herself to go to the bathroom, and when she comes out she sees Katheryn rubbing Russell's back as a look of panic flashes across his face.

IN HER ROOM at Parkside, she lifts the phone receiver and dials, hears three rings, then a click and the sound of her own voice. "You have reached the Recording Room's dictation mailbox. Please note that this voice mailbox has a maximum duration of twenty minutes . . ."

Resting the receiver like an infant against her shoulder, she stands and listens to the sound of her muffled voice, then the universal tone.

"Arlene," she says, picking up the receiver and cradling it against her ear, "it's me."

She pauses; it is so quiet she thinks she can hear the tape turn, but maybe it's true that when there are no sounds, the brain can make them up. She thinks of the empty Recording Room, the panel of phones, the archaic overnight machine, the televisions, the empty desks, her desk, her chair, the window, and, on the ledge, the pigeon.

"How do people just vanish? There's a foreign reporter with a modest, reliable voice. I look forward to his calls. He called in a story about the mudslide in Pakistan. But he never called back with the rest of the story. And when I asked Russell about it, he said, 'Eric knows how to take care of himself.' But what has that got to do with anything? So many things go unrecorded, Arlene. So many things are lost."

CHAPTER SIX

Chaucer's Scrivener Revealed

In the morning she goes for a walk, a Saturday morning ritual, and something in Madison Square Park catches her eye; she watches, motionless. A falcon holds a pigeon in its talons and tears into it as the pigeon still struggles with life. She can't move. God, eaten alive. She remembers reading that falcons are capable of diving for prey at two hundred miles an hour. And that they can knock a bird out in flight, then swoop underneath to catch it falling.

What did Arlene feel the moment the lions' teeth first

tore her skin? It is one thing to kill yourself, and another to have someone else do it, and still another to give yourself to teeth and hunger that know no judgment, no free will. And it is even something else when the killers themselves are confined to cages where people can come and watch them live.

ON THE WAY back to Parkside, she pauses by a deli to watch a man cutting flowers to sell. The funereal lilies give off their sweet, cloying scent, the irises' beauty is already beginning to fade, the elegant tulips stand tall on slender stalks. Lena looks at the gerbera daisies, bright, fat, and gay, and reaches for a bunch, then suddenly changes her mind and picks a bouquet of yellow roses.

The Salvation Army is quiet; Mrs. Pelletier sits behind her desk, her glasses hang from a chain around her neck, her hands cover her eyes. Lena pauses, and Mrs. Pelletier sits up straight, puts her glasses on carefully, placing both plastic arms securely behind her ears.

"Yes, Ms. Respass?"

"Good morning, Mrs. Pelletier. No matter what time I come in or go out, you seem to always be at your post."

"No rest for the weary, Ms. Respass."

Lena lifts the roses and holds them through the partition. "These are for you. I thought they might brighten things up a bit."

"Why, Ms. Respass," she says, half rising, "that is . . . this is"—she pauses, feeling speechless, something she does not like to feel—"not necessary."

"Oh, of course, it's not necessary. I just thought it might be nice to have fresh flowers—"

"But Ms. Respass—"

"—in the reception area."

"I see. Well, of course, if it's for the *reception area* I suppose it might be nice to, as you say, brighten things up a bit."

"Yes. I think the residents would like to be greeted with flowers."

"I see. Well, of course, it's not necessary," she says, reaching through the window for the flowers and placing them on the counter. "But I'm sure the girls will appreciate it." She leans over, pressing her hand to her chest as if to close a gaping blouse, and smells the roses with her eyes closed.

"I'm sorry," Lena says. "They don't have much scent."

"Oh, well, everything fades."

Lena nods and considers the remark, since the deli roses never had any scent to lose. The scent has been bred out, she starts to say, then thinks better of it.

"Mrs. Pelletier, do you have a phone book?"

"Yes, of course, Ms. Respass. Do you want the yellow pages or the white?"

"White, please."

Mrs. Pelletier disappears below the counter and re-appears with the bulky book. "There's something so satisfying about a phone book, isn't there?" she asks, patting the book's cover. "Such a useful book, so full of names. It's exactly the information you need and nothing more. No waste."

"Yes." Lena opens the pulpy-paged thing, and Mrs. Pelletier hesitates, as if to say something else, but instead goes to her desk and leaves Lena alone with the names.

She flips to *L* and turns pages, passing hundreds of New Yorkers by: Label, Labov, Ladyrinth, Laflamme, Laitman, Lamardore, Landberg, Landis—faster—Lanyard, Lazarus, Lear, Leazard, Lebidois, Lebin, Leblanc, Leblanche, Leblang, Lebleu, Leboeuf, Lebonitte, Lebosco, Lebot, Lebous, Lebovits, Lebovitz, Lebow . . . Armand, Benita, Bennett, Colin, Earl, Ellen. Ellen Lebow. She writes down the Upper West Side address and closes the book with a slapping sound.

"Thank you."

Waiting for the elevator, she turns back. Mrs. Pelletier sits at her desk, staring at her hands. The harsh lights thrum faintly overhead, the fake glass window waits to be closed and locked, a round white-faced clock like those in public schools hangs on the wall, and Mrs. Pelletier sits at her station, wearing a brown skirt two inches below the knee and a crepe de chine blouse that ties in a droopy bow at the neck. The scene could be a diorama at the Natural History Museum, where years ago an anthropologist kept several Inuit in the basement for study. When four of them died, the bodies were dissected and kept in the museum. Even after one man's son discovered that his father's bones were on display, he was not able to claim them. A museum where children play and shriek at dinosaurs, and a place where a boy's father is displayed behind glass and his son has no rights to his bones.

In her room, she stares at the slip of paper with Ellen's address and asks herself what a detective would do. She knows no detectives but she has read Chandler and Hammett, so she gets the Jack Daniel's from underneath the socks in the top dresser drawer. She washes her one glass, the one holding her toothbrush, and pours. There is no ice, so when she shakes the glass it makes no sound. She sips, swallows, breathes with her mouth open.

She dresses carefully, black linen pants and a sleeveless top, espadrilles bought in Chinatown. Since it's a special occasion, she puts on lipstick, called Damned. She remembers the way her mother did it, before church on Sunday: Wearing one of her four dresses, she would open her mouth and tuck her lips over her teeth so that she appeared toothless and widemouthed, which is how she looked when she died at the age of forty-three of the disease the name of which is still whispered by a certain generation in a certain part of the country. Pink in the

Afternoon, the only shade she ever owned, in a gold tube, the only bright gold thing in the house. Lena has never mastered the art of application and wipes around her mouth with a tissue.

IN FRONT OF the gray prewar building at 112th Street and Riverside Drive, she paces up and down the block, clutching her *Record* ID in her hand and rehearsing what she will say. She takes her newly purchased recorder out of her bag and tests it three times, even though she has tested it several times before.

Finally she forces herself to stop outside Ellen's building and, after finding "E. Lebow" on the metal intercom, she presses the button for apartment 7E.

"Hello?" a voice says over the door-speaker static.

"Hello, is this Ellen Lebow? I'm Lena Respass from the *Record*. May I talk with you?"

There is no response, only a long pause and then the sound of the buzzer, the sound of entry, of arrival, of expectation, of being buzzed in. To Lena, the sound is that of the starting bell that begins a race, and her heart lurches as she opens the door and enters the lobby. On the seventh floor, she knocks on Ellen's door, and as soon as it opens, she presents her ID like a badge, but the woman just smiles and ushers her inside.

She leads Lena down a book-lined hallway to a spacious room, the living room of an academic whose field has fallen from favor: parquet floors; a comfortable, cushiony sofa covered with a red Turkish throw; more bookshelves; paintings of dark landscapes; and a white cat balancing on one of the clawed feet of a heavy dining table. It could be a theater set for an academic's apartment.

"I'm Lena. Thank you for agreeing to speak with me."

"I'm Ellen. You're working on the weekend?"

"The news is relentless."

Ellen removes her glasses, and Lena sees that she is an attractive woman, fiftysomething, with the tired eyes of a constant reader.

"So, what do you want to know?"

"Oh, anything you want to tell me."

"Well, mainly I'm surprised that no one found it before."

"What do you mean?"

"It was so simple, really, hiding in plain sight."

Lena has no idea how to respond. It must be a mistake, a misunderstanding, she thinks as she looks out the big windows that overlook the Hudson. The sky is white, bleached bright, stripped of clouds.

"It was in the handwriting," Ellen says. "I compared his signature on the scrivener's register with the signature on the manuscript."

"Pardon?"

"That's how I discovered the name of Chaucer's copyist, his scrivener."

"I'm sorry—Chaucer. You thought I was here about Chaucer?"

"That's not why you wanted to talk to me?"

"I wanted to talk to you about your sister, Arlene."

"Oh," Ellen says, touching her throat. "I thought you were here about my discovery."

"I'm happy to hear about it," Lena says quickly, feeling weak. If there was a point at which she could turn back, she has passed it. She is an impostor. Strangely, this makes her feel more confident, and she smiles encouragingly at Ellen just as she has imagined reporters doing countless times while she has transcribed their interviews.

"Oh, I should have known. It's just that Arlene's story is over, that's done now. The *Record* reporter I spoke with, he said they wouldn't bother me anymore. And the university issued a release about my academic discovery just yesterday, and the press, well, some press, mainly British, of course, have been contacting me to ask about it. So you see—"

"Of course. Please, start with Chaucer. What were you saying—you found Chaucer's copyist?"

The excitement comes back into her eyes, erasing the fatigue. "Yes. I discovered the identity of Chaucer's scrivener, which helps certify Chaucer's work. He had written a poem about Adam—are you sure you're interested?"

"Yes, please, go on. I have a personal interest in scriveners. And an editor at the *Record* might be interested."

"Oh, but someone at the *Record* has already called."

Lena smiles and swallows what seems to be sweat in her mouth. "That would be culture. I'm with metro."

"I see. Well, besides being Arlene's sister, I'm a Chaucer scholar. I'd been on the trail for quite a while and I finally compared the two signatures. The evidence has been there for centuries, but I suppose no one had looked for it before."

"And how did you know which scrivener to look for?"

"Chaucer had written a poem about him, criticizing his mistakes and threatening to curse him with scabs."

"Was he incompetent?"

"No, not at all. In fact, I think he was Chaucer's favorite. But it's a strange relationship between an author and his copyist. This was a time when writers were still working closely with individual scribes and relied on them tremendously. Later, the scriptoria became the standard. But it was one man, Adam the scrivener, who noted Chaucer's death in the tales, letting us know that Chaucer died before he finished them."

"How did he do it?"

"He put a line right in the text saying Chaucer had written no more of the tale," she says, stroking the cat, which has left its perch under the table and is now stalking the tabletop as if on a runway, "a copyist's code that we might find hundreds of years later."

"I wonder how he felt, an anonymous scrivener announcing Chaucer's death in print, inserting his obit in his own text."

"It was a tribute. And as someone who works for a newspaper, you must see how we are all dependent on public recognition. Now we have—come here, look at this," she says, gently pushing the cat away and crossing the room to the computer on a scroll-top desk. "I've created a database of scribes in fourteenth- and fifteenth-century England."

She pages down the screen and there are the rescued names of the scribes of England. "Do you know anything else about them?" Lena asks.

"No, only their names. What else can we know?"

"I wonder if any of the others added or omitted anything from the texts they copied. There were so many, it seems unlikely that Adam was the only one."

"I wonder about that, too," Ellen says. "There were so many manuscripts to be copied; a codex was such a laborious object to produce. Not like now, when we're drowning in words."

"It's true. There's entirely too much writing. 'When did we write so much as since our dissensions began? When did the Romans write so much as in the time of their downfall?' "

"Excuse me?"

"Montaigne. I'm sorry. I quote a lot, it's a bad habit I'm trying to quit."

"Ah. Well, here, let's sit down." She gestures toward the couch. "You're here about Arlene. What did you want to know?"

The cat leaps onto Ellen's lap and they both look at the animal, which, sensing the shift in attention, swishes its tail with elaborate slowness.

"To be honest, I don't know that the *Record* will run another story about Arlene. But if I had more information, I could pitch something to an editor. So, whatever you want to tell me would be helpful."

"About her blindness?"

"More about her life."

"You seem remarkably patient for a reporter. You haven't been doing this long, have you?"

"No, I'm quite new to it. It's also—I've taken a personal interest in Arlene."

"Why?"

"I can't explain it."

"She used to say that she didn't have a blind spot.

Funny the things you remember. I didn't know what she meant, but it always stayed with me. She said seeing people have blind spots and she didn't."

"Was she"—Lena pauses, unable to find the word—"happy?"

Ellen shrugs. "She wasn't always unhappy. Then she was. Things tend to catch up."

"Yes, they do. Was she blind from childhood?"

"No. She went blind at the age of nineteen, when she had meningitis. What exactly are you looking for, Lena?"

Lena looks down at her hands, unable to answer.

"It's nice to talk about her, I mean other than as a news story, to remember her. Our parents are gone, we didn't have a large family. So, go ahead, ask what you want."

"Did she work?"

"Yes. She was a court reporter."

"Really?" Lena says, trying to act surprised, though of course she remembers that Arlene told her that. "So we're both transcriptionists."

"What do you mean? Newspaper reporters and court reporters aren't the same thing at all."

"Of course. I transcribe my own interviews though. It always takes longer than you think it will."

She puts the tape recorder between them on the coffee table. It had taken a great deal of time for her to choose it, and she had tried the patience of the clerk at the electronics store, who kept telling her that tapes would soon be obsolete and she should consider the new digital recorders, which were smaller and lighter and could store a "tremendous amount of data." She had tried to explain to him that she didn't deal in data and couldn't transcribe interviews on a digital recorder because she used a Dictaphone, but he didn't know what a Dictaphone was. Even with the minicassette recorder she will have to use the one Dictaphone that plays minicassettes and for some mysterious reason never works as well as the machines that play regular-size cassettes.

"Do you mind if I turn this on?"

"That's fine. I'm surprised you waited so long. Where were we? Arlene was not reporting, she was recording. She was transcribing exactly what other people were saying, all day, every day. It was a very difficult job—I mean, not only the work, the concentration, the, well, submission to listening to people's tragedies all day. It was very difficult for her to get the job in the first place. No one had ever heard of a blind court reporter. She had to use a special dictatype machine. She worked extremely hard, and when she passed the exam she was still in her twenties. So she had been absorbing the trials and tribulations of others for years. But she said it wasn't the murders that finally got to her. It was after she moved to family court, the custody battles, the hideousness of family relations. I could see that she was getting sadder, but it happened gradually. I didn't know that she had passed from sorrow to futility."

Lena tries to hide her disconcertment: She and Arlene, both professional listeners, recorders. The recognition between them had been real. She accepts this, though she cannot explain it and knows it is not reasonable.

"Did she ever enjoy the work?"

"At first I think she did. But eventually it began to take quite a toll, more than I knew. I remember a conversation we had some months ago about the case she was working on. It was a fraught trial, very sad; a woman was accused of having her husband murdered while they were divorcing and fighting over custody of their daughter. They played a recording in court of the child screaming—"roaring," as Arlene called it—as she was being delivered from one parent to the other. Arlene was distraught over this tape, she said she couldn't transcribe it, there were no words, and after, she couldn't get away from the sound of the screams. She was also upset that the recording was made in the first place. One parent had secretly recorded the child to show that she didn't want to go with the other parent. Something about that bothered Arlene tremendously."

In this moment, Lena sees Ellen's likeness to her sister, the startling sadness of the smile, a fullness, a shapeliness of the lips. And her hands, the same elegant, elongated fingers. Lena reaches out and puts her hand on Ellen's, stops herself from stroking the back of it.

"Do you think it bothered her—and maybe this

isn't even true—do you think it bothered her that her work, transcription, is becoming obsolete, that machines will soon do all the listening, that her work was losing meaning?"

"Well, I suppose I'm fortunate that Chaucer lost his major audience ages ago," Ellen says, gently moving her hand. "But for Arlene, I would think technology was much more an opportunity than a defeat. It's you as a newspaper reporter who suffer the loss of meaning in the world's eyes."

"That's probably true."

"What else do you want to know?"

"Did she leave a note?"

"Not with her, not that they found. The truth is, I haven't been to her apartment yet. I just can't. But I don't believe there's anything there, I think I know her well enough to know she wouldn't leave anything behind."

Lena is disgusted with herself; she is picking through Arlene's bones. People might be pathetically easy to find, but sometimes they don't want to be found.

"I'm sorry, Ellen. I'm intruding," she says, standing. "I should leave. But if there's anything I can do . . ."

"I would like to do for her what Adam did for Chaucer. I know she lived a hidden life, but her death was newsworthy. I'd like to see an obit in the *Record*."

"The paid death notices are handled by classified advertising. I can give you their number."

"No, I meant an obit, a tribute, in the A section of the paper, after the news, written by a staff writer."

"I'm sorry, Ellen. I can't do that. The obits are decided by the editors based on news value."

Ellen nods. "News value. That says it all, then."

"One last question, I have to ask. Why lions?"

"We'll never know. But she loved to sit in the zoo, listening for the lions. She said hearing them was like being punctured by sound, like being released. And she was an excellent swimmer. Everybody is so surprised about that part, but you can swim with your eyes closed. Who swims with their eyes open? We're all blind underwater."

THAT NIGHT IN her room, she calls the overnight machine. "Arlene, I went to see your sister today. I don't know if I should have gone. And it didn't make me feel any closer to you. I felt closer to you this morning, when I saw a falcon devour a pigeon. It was in Madison Square Park, that odd little pocket of space. As I approached the William Seward statue, the forgotten abolitionist, there was a quietness, a stillness, and a few isolated sounds, a gasp, a curse, a question. I paused and heard someone say, 'It's a falcon. He's got a pigeon. The pigeon is—oh God, the pigeon is alive, he's struggling. Oh.' We all stood motionless, honoring the pigeon, the falcon, a life ending before us. I could see the falcon holding the humble bird in its talons and tearing into it as the pigeon still pulsed with life. We watched in awe and wonder; it seemed a very dignified death, though probably not to the pigeon. It was shocking to see nature assert itself in the middle of Manhattan. We stood together in excitement and I thought of Aquinas: *The saved would feast on the sight of the sufferings of the damned.* But who are the saved, Arlene, and who are the damned?

"The week my mother died, the church congregation came to anoint her head with oil. I suppose some of them must have thought it would help, but it was an irrevocable invasion of privacy. I was in her bedroom watching from the window as they came toward the house. I watched as they crossed the gravel drive and opened the door without knocking. My father met them in the kitchen and led them down the hall.

"I turned away from the light outside toward my mother, who was propped up in bed.

" 'Why?' I said. 'Why are you letting them do this to you?'

"She smiled wanly and said, 'It couldn't hurt.' That's what she said, 'It couldn't hurt.' She could have meant several things by that. And when she said it, she had this expression that I have never seen again, except the day I saw you on the bus."

CHAPTER SEVEN

Lions Upset after
Mauling Woman to Death

At the newsstand, she picks up the *Record* and puts it down. She looks at the front page of the *Post* and *Daily News* and stops in front of the *Financial Times*. The *Financial Times*. She might have a different life if she read the *Financial Times*. It's too late. She buys the *Record* and goes to a neighborhood coffee shop where a group of Italian men, regulars, sit under the green awning.

"Why the hell you so dressed up?" one of the group says to a recent arrival. The speaker has thick, pearly-gray hair swept to the side. It is his pride and joy, and he pats it often, afraid it may jump up and skitter away.

"I'm not dressed up," the man replies, pleased with this deviation from the daily routine. "I've just got on a polo shirt."

They begin to discuss whether they would rather have been born rich or handsome. This debate is taken up periodically and will last all morning.

Lena sits down at the table next to them and sorts the *Record* by section.

"The six-pound Sunday *Record*," one of the men says, "the white man's burden."

She scans the front page, reads about Greek sailors who have been detained as witnesses of "environmental crimes." The men are living in a hotel near Kennedy Airport, and every afternoon, they pack their single duffel bags and sit in the parking lot waiting for the shipping company to pay that day's hotel bill so they can check back in. This is the only time they venture outside, because their passports have been taken and they are, as one sailor says, "100 percent illegal."

They spend their days watching television and waiting and eating food from the vending machines.

"The hard part is not knowing when we can leave," one man says. "It is a little like living at sea. But only the bad parts. The hotel is like a ship but we are not moving. We are living at sea without the sea. We cannot leave. We must wait." They have been in the hotel for four months.

Waiting.

She is almost at the subway before she realizes where she is going. But first, she pauses before a small shop that sells colorful cotton dresses, silver jewelry, incense, bags made from flour sacks, flat-soled espadrilles, and, by the door, what always catches her eye, a round rack of long, lightweight scarves.

She pushes the door open and a bell jangles. She smiles at the old-fashioned touch. An Indian woman in a pink-and-gold sari smiles at her from behind the register.

"Hello."

A beautiful brown-eyed boy stares around the counter at her, clutching a fistful of sari.

"Hello there."

"Pow!" he yells as he fires his toy pistol.

"America," his mother says by way of explanation.

"Ah," Lena says. She begins to look through the dresses. "China," she adds, glancing at a dress tag. The message on the square brown tag has mistakes that make her read it twice.

"The occasional irregularity in shading and weaving are characteristic of the cloth. Each and every piece is as individual and extinct as you are. They are not to be treated as defects. MADE IN CHINA."

She holds out a yellow sundress with three embroidered star-shaped flowers along the neckline. When she sees the flowers, she puts it back on the rack.

"It's pretty," the woman says, coming from behind the counter. "It would look pretty with your hair."

Lena touches her hair; it used to be the color of fire ants, but lately it has faded to diluted gasoline. She nods, smiles, moves to the scarf rack.

"You are married?"

"No."

"Boyfriend?"

"No."

"Maybe with the yellow dress you'll find someone."

She nods again and looks at the scarves. They hang from wire racks, and she touches them, running her hand down the length of them, looking for flaws in the fragile silk. Dark green and orange, black, blue, pink, purple. She picks out a brown one: it is bright like the boy's eyes.

She pays for it and turns to go. "Thank you." She opens the door, the bell sounds, she turns back.

"I'll take the dress after all."

"Good," the woman says, quickly retrieving it from the rack. "Maybe it will bring you luck. Maybe you will find someone."

AT THE ZOO, she takes her time, locating the lion area immediately on the map, then avoiding it, saving it for last, the way she would a treat or a chore. She watches the polar bears, shaggy and tatty furred, then the sea lions, who stare with woeful eyes and swim toward her, bumping the glass. There is something both mortal and meditative in their circular swimming, across the pool, around the rock, bump the glass, across and around again.

She wanders toward the lions and sits on the most distant bench, where she can see the entire enclosure. A class of camp kids in bright orange T-shirts crowds in front of the railing.

"I swear they're multiplying," one ponytailed counselor says to another as she counts heads. "Are you sure we haven't picked up a few from Lake George?"

The lions stretch lazily in the sun and gaze indifferently at their observers. Then, looking directly at the children as if to give them their money's worth, one of them roars. The children shriek and scamper, then are through. Someone wants to see snakes, others want ice cream.

One boy—he looks seven or eight—stands slightly apart and grips the handrail that separates the moat from the pavement. He has a long, narrow face, a large head out of proportion with his lanky frame. He watches the lions, mesmerized. The other kids jump around the camp counselors, giving ice cream orders noisily, so it is Lena who witnesses the boy begin to scream.

The lions look at him idly; one swishes his tail languorously. The boy screams again, louder, holding the iron rail with both hands. The sound contains both yawp and provocation, tones of fear and longing.

"Bobby!" a camp counselor shouts. "Bobby White!"

The boy doesn't seem to hear but lifts a sandaled foot onto the railing, which is above his waist.

"What are you doing?" the counselor says, snatching his arm. He doesn't move when she grabs him, and she lets go in surprise, her empty hand pausing in the air.

There is something strange in the child's behavior, something unsettling. The counselor squats down and speaks gently.

"What's wrong, Bobby? He can't get you. He's over there, see? Don't be frightened, he can't get you."

Bobby covers his ears and presses his hands against his head; his long face seems to grow even longer. "He's roaring."

"He's not roaring," the counselor says, pulling Bobby's hands away from his ears. "You're imagining it. See, listen."

"But I hear him," Bobby says, almost whimpering.

"No," the counselor says. "He's not roaring."

Bobby holds the railing with both hands, and the frazzled counselor must pry his fingers away one by one.

"I hear it, too," Lena says.

But the counselor is dragging Bobby off. He goes silently, with his head turned, watching the lions.

I seem forsaken and alone,
I hear the lion roar;

She tries to remember the rest.

And every door is shut but one,
And that is Mercy's door.

The roar comes again; the sound is a steel thread that glides straight through her, the needle's eye threaded by an unseen hand. The lion is expressionless, as if he has been instructed by his master to sing from behind the mask. He'll never lose that voice, she thinks, but I'm losing mine. It's happening. Her voice is fading, being replaced by others, the ones recorded on endless tapes, and now, the lion's roar. Like the voice imitator who imitates anyone upon request but when asked to imitate himself is unable.

She walks to the railing and stands where Bobby White stood and where Arlene must have stood. She grips it tighter, and her palms moisten the metal with sweat.

In kindergarten, she went on a class field trip to a petting zoo. It was mainly goats and chickens and it smelled awful. Most of the children got a bacterial infection. The teacher explained to Lena's mother that she didn't get it because she didn't pet the animals. She observed them from behind the fence and felt sorry for them because they did not have a place to hide from onlookers like her.

She looks down at the railing, at her two ordinary hands, which type and type and type every day. She is an anonymous transcriptionist who does not know the separateness of suicide or know the separateness of the lions. Looking at them, she wonders whether they keep the memory of killing, even though they are blameless. It is their nature. Maybe that is why they kill in the first place: they carry the memory of killing from their ancestors, even after a lifetime at the zoo.

The sun feels warm, as if coffee is being poured just under her skin, and she wanders to a shady spot under some oak trees. There is a trailer office between the trees and the bathrooms, a reminder of the labor behind all this artificial nature. She walks up the plywood steps to the trailer and knocks on the door, which is opened by a young man who clearly moved here from somewhere else not long ago.

"Yes?"

"Hi. I'm from the *Record*," she says, fumbling in her bag for her ID, which she holds out awkwardly. "May I ask you a few questions about the woman who was killed in the lions' den?"

"Oh. I don't know if I can help you. I mean, I've only been here two months; I'm just a guard."

"A guard?" She tries to look kind and encouraging, benign.

"Yeah, I just sit in the trailer and watch surveillance tapes."

"Really? You must see a lot."

He shakes his head. "It's boring, actually. I see a lot of kids trying to shove candy into cages, a lot of temper tantrums. That's about it."

"Is it air-conditioned inside? Could I come in, just for a few minutes?"

He moves aside so that she can enter. "Well, I guess so. I should be sitting in front of the monitors anyway."

The room is dimly lit and smells of chemical carpet fiber and electronic equipment kept in a closed space. Two rows of video monitors line the shelves behind the metal desk.

"It's the matinee," he says.

People cross the screens as if in a black-and-white dream, doing banal things without a sound, pointing over a fence, pausing at a fork in the path. A child drops an ice cream cone and begins to cry.

"It's so boring," he says. "I never noticed growing up in Iowa, but now people seem so much the same. Day after day, same, same, same. Buy the ice cream, eat the ice cream or drop the ice cream. Cry over the ice cream."

"Do you monitor the entire zoo or a specific section?"

"I have this section," he says, pointing. "The top row shows the path and the bathrooms. These screens on the bottom row show the lion area, but you can't really see the lions, just the benches and railings by the moat."

They look at the screens; the mute people seem displaced, with no past or future, suspended in surveillance. Then they disappear.

"So, you're a reporter for the *Record*."

"Hmm."

"That must be cool. You get to go out and do stuff and not be cooped up all day."

"Sometimes. But there's a lot of sitting at a desk in front of a screen, like you. Anyway, I wanted to ask you about the woman who was killed. Do you have video from that night?"

"No. I probably shouldn't tell you this, but the cameras near the lions' den weren't working when the woman was killed. Besides, we don't leave them on overnight anyway."

"You don't?"

"No, at least we didn't. There's nobody here at night except the animals. And they get on fine without us. It's the people we have to watch."

"Did you hear anything about what happened?"

"Well, it was awful for the lions really. How can they be happy now?"

On the monitors, people pass in noiseless movement. She wonders whether they would act differently if they knew they were being watched. Or maybe most people assume they're being watched now.

"The lions aren't happy?"

"They're very upset. They can't settle down. It's like before they forgot they were in a cage, but now they've remembered where they are. They've tasted blood and they just can't settle down."

"Are the ones out there today the same ones that killed her?"

"Some of them, but one, Robert, had to be taken out. He's relaxing at a retreat upstate—Cullen Sanctuary in Hudson. Poor Robert, the woman who's taking care of him says he acts like his heart is broken. I don't know, maybe he feels bad for killing that woman. But what could he do? He's a lion."

She looks at the square screens. Maybe she should be a surveillance-screen watcher. She already knows how to be anonymously present at all kinds of places. Maybe the transcription of images would be more interesting. She knows how to listen neutrally and record words on a page, but it is something else to watch offensively, looking for suspicious gestures lurking in the everyday.

There are no answers for her here. She had allowed herself to be distracted by the familiar scene of a room recording snippets of the outside world. But there is nothing true to be found about Arlene on a surveillance screen.

She thanks the guard for his time. He spells his name twice so that she'll be sure to get it right in the *Record*. It's an investigative piece, she tells him, hard to say when it will be published. He tells her she can visit again if she wants. It is very hard to sit inside all day, he says, alone in a room watching people who don't talk.

Outside, she feels a surge of lightness, and at the fork in the path she looks up at the surveillance eye secured to a utility pole. For a few moments she blinks slowly, then steps closer, feeling the force of her gaze. She lifts her hand to wave, but blows a kiss instead.

THE SUBWAY PLATFORM is smelly, sweaty, dank as a tomb. Across the platform, the uptown tracks are closed off and three men with helmet lights walk the tracks. "We call him feathers," one man says to the other. "You know why? Because he's a chicken." They all laugh and move like miners along the rails.

The downtown train roars into the station and she breaks into a sweat. It is scalp sweat, the sweat of fear. A toddler covers her ears as her mother pulls her by the elbow through the open train doors. Lena is shaking when she steps into the train car, and she turns back; she needs to get out, she cannot breathe. As she steps toward the door she locks eyes with the child who is still covering her ears; she looks at Lena with eyes like whirlpools of light blue. The train doors close just as Lena is about to step off, and she presses her palms against the door as the train carries her away from the lions.

THAT NIGHT SHE has her recurring nightmare: Dirty streets filled with charred feet and bloated bodies. They have been banished from the world by editors, and this is where they disappear to, her dreams, which have become a decayed landscape, a landfill of edited things. She gathers them up in her arms and runs through the streets, trying to find their owners, who will know the dismembered limbs and the forgotten words. She runs with her arms full, and the streets become Manhattan streets in some terrible future that seems like now, west to the Hudson River, and there, like a ghost ship, is the ship of Crete. It comes toward her, gliding fast on dream water, and there is loud creaking and clanking as the anchor is let down and the ship is secured not with ropes but with chains. It is then that she realizes this is the only sound, and she turns back toward a silent city. Men without faces wordlessly lift the remains from her arms and load them onto the ship, then drift off into the river, which has widened behind them and turned into a black-blue sea.

Lena awakens and, unable to fall back to sleep, lies in the dark and presses the wall behind her head. Arlene's face is starting to fade from memory. She thinks of getting up and finding the clipping with Arlene's photo, but she wants to retrieve the memory, how she saw her that day on the bus. The only image she can conjure is a composite of lion sketches and Patience and Fortitude and the lion roaring in the zoo and the child with the narrow face.

She hears the click, then the sound of the tape worming around the spool. "Stop torturing me," she says. Reaching out, she touches the phone with her hand, sits up, and dials the Recording Room.

"Arlene? It's Lena. I went to the zoo. I saw the moat. How did you swim that, Arlene? Could you hear the lions waiting for you?

"I wish I had stayed with you on the bus that day. I wish I could have helped you. When I left the academic cloister, I thought the Recording Room would be insulation from the world. But it's not. It's too difficult to eat the news with my ears every day. It leaves a residue. I have letters in my bloodstream, nut graphs in my gut, headlines around my heart. It usurps my soul. You knew about that. But people don't understand, do they? We have to listen. We have to accept them into our bodies. People have no regard for what their stories do.

"Arlene, my body is merging with the newspaper. I'm losing myself. First, I lost myself to Scripture when I was a child, and then to literature when I was a little older, and now the news, which is the worst of all. It has replaced everything; all the words of suffering keep flowing through my veins. But I have to separate myself. It's just as you said. We can't keep up with the suffering."

She hangs up and lies back against the pillow. The shadowy furniture, the bureau, the desk, and the white sink seem to float in the darkness. The imaginary tape spools quietly in the dark, but the voice does not begin. She involuntarily pumps the invisible foot pedal as if to forward to the place where the voice starts. But it does not come.

CHAPTER EIGHT

Massacre in Mideast; Hope Turns to Despair

As Lena is walking to work in the morning, a woman suddenly grabs her arm and points up to a balcony across the street.

"She's not going to jump, is she?"

Lena looks up at the open window, where she can see the variegated leaf of a plant draped like a weary arm over the sill.

"Oh, she's gone away," the woman says, and for the first time she looks Lena in the eye. She is a middle-aged woman whose face has permanent traces of anxiety and alarm. "I'm so afraid of heights now, I can't open my windows."

Before Lena can respond, the woman is gone, swallowed up in the pedestrian sea. She continues along the avenue, looking up, hearing snippets of conversation, and twitching her fingers to transcribe them on air.

"The super said he gave it a kiss and a prayer."

"Why, in Russian you have to move your lips more?"

"Can you hear me? I can see you."

Approaching Times Square, she feels a thread of sweat along the small of her back. She steps into the street to skirt the tourists who have already crowded the corner to examine tables of handbags and socks and old jazz magazines and albums. The men selling—it is nearly always men with these wares—have boom boxes and canvas butterfly chairs and coolers.

IN THE RECORD'S elevator, she remembers that today is escape-hood training. The paper has canceled all holiday parties this year and instead has invested in escape hoods, four thousand of them for seventy dollars each. Employees have received offers to buy escape hoods for family members at this same generous discount.

She glances at today's front page. Children are working as rock crushers in Kenya. A young boy and his father have to pass the family's one pencil off to each other—

one takes it to school in the morning, one takes it to work in the evening. Soldiers killed in Iraq, civilians killed in Afghanistan, monks killed in Myanmar, lawyers killed in Pakistan. A mysterious weed is choking swamps in Louisiana. Scientists have discovered that moths in Madagascar drink the tears of sleeping birds.

The Recording Room phone is silent. She lingers with the paper, reading about people in China who are arrested and encouraged to confess. There must be a transcriptionist in China who specializes in confessions. There must be hundreds. The confessor's cries that arise from the "encouragement" must be off the record.

She begins to pace. At these moments, when she has gorged on too many sad stories, she has such a longing to create something, to produce something, to bring forth something, or to commit some violence, that she considers ripping the articles from the paper just to destroy the paper itself. But she doesn't. Really she is afraid of committing any violent act, even against paper, because it reminds her that she never knows where the drop-off point is, but she does know that it takes only a second to step over it.

She glances at the paper again, and a sentence catches her eye. "More graves are believed to exist, but no one is willing to reveal their locations."

There is a knock on the door, which she opens to find a science reporter and a rabbi standing side by side.

"We'd like to make a copy of this videotape," the reporter says.

"Of course, come in. I can copy it for you and call you when it's done."

"I thought we'd stay and watch it, if you don't mind."

"You might not want to stay," the rabbi says to Lena. "It's a video of a kosher slaughterhouse."

"It's okay. I'll just sit back here and do my work."

She inserts the original and a blank videotape into the side-by-side VCRs and places chairs in front of the TVs so that they can watch. At her desk, she puts on her headphones and pumps the foot pedal to make the empty tape unwind so that she can pretend to work.

On the TV screen, which she has a clear view of, a steer's throat is slit. A worker pulls something out of its neck with a hook and the steer falls to the floor. The animal stands up shakily as pinkish-white throat muscles hang exposed.

"Is that pain?" the rabbi asks the reporter. "Who are we to say he feels something?"

Another steer is slit, hooked, and dumped on the slimy floor. Lena sits in silence, headphones on, staring. She has never seen slaughter, except in childhood on the farm, when she saw only the aftermath.

The science reporter is quiet, fidgety. The rabbi talks

in a monotonous voice used to comfort witnesses to the dead.

"What causes unconsciousness?" he asks. "Blood loss. The shohet has slit the throat, and this man here"—he touches the screen with his finger, emitting the faintest buzz of static—"has removed the trachea. Blood pressure has been lost. Have you ever seen a snake with its head chopped off?"

"No."

"Well, you get the concept."

"Yes."

"Sometimes they continue to move, but not for long. Chickens, too. It's involuntary movement."

The reporter nods.

The rabbi turns to Lena as another steer falls to the floor. "I didn't invite you to watch," he says softly, the voice of absolution.

She blushes and pumps the foot pedal. "Qwerty," she types, "pain and consciousness."

She cannot look away from the screen where steers flail on the bloody floor while the rabbi speaks about humane death.

"We do not believe in drugging the animal before it is killed," the rabbi says.

"Another shehitah expert said the first cut must cause instant unconsciousness," the reporter says.

"What is consciousness?"

"You're the rabbi. How can there be so much argument about it?"

"We have no pope," the rabbi says with a smile.

ONCE THE SLAUGHTERHOUSE pair leaves, she cannot settle down at her desk. She paces the room and stacks and restacks the cassette tapes in the cardboard box. The tape with the lead from Eric Isaacs about the mudslide is still unclaimed. She rewinds it on the recording Dictaphone and plays it out loud.

" 'The earth shook, then I felt mud in my mouth.'

". . . so much mud . . . fear that some bodies will not be found . . .

". . . said they would be back digging the next day, and the next, and the day after that, and for as long as it would take to find her.

" 'We will not leave anyone behind,' he said. 'That is not our way.' "

She searches Eric Isaacs's name on the Web. On the *Record*'s site, his bylined articles appear consistently until a week ago. There has been nothing since then, and of the three articles on the mudslide, one is by a stringer and the other two are wire stories. She reads Eric's skeletal bio on Wikipedia: it lists his birthdate and his education and notes that he came to the *Record* in 1998, after winning a Pulitzer for his coverage of the Taliban for the *Washington Post*.

She paces the room some more, and when she sits down at her computer again and presses "refresh," Eric's Wikipedia page has disappeared. She refreshes again and again, but it is not there.

"KOV?" SHE CALLS softly. "Kov?"

He opens the door and ushers her inside without a word.

"The strangest thing just happened. Eric Isaacs called in a story about the mudslide in Pakistan a few days ago. But he only dictated the lead, he never called back with the rest of the story. The story ran with a stringer's byline. Eric hasn't had a story since then. And just now, I was looking at his Wikipedia page and it disappeared."

"Lena, Eric has been kidnapped."

"What?"

"He did the mudslide story because he was already in the area. He was crossing into Waziristan for an interview with a Taliban leader. The *Record* and the Isaacs family have asked other news organizations to cooperate, even Wikipedia, in keeping it private. They think if his kidnapping is publicized, he'll be in more danger."

"How do you know all this?"

"I've been here a lifetime. I still hear what's going on."

"Do you think it's the right response, to keep silent?"

"It's what the *Record* and the family have decided, so I don't have to approve it, only to respect it."

"Is there anything we can do?"

"Wait. People are trying to help, but right now we can only wait."

There is a peck at the window. Kov crosses the room, raises the window. A pigeon struts across the windowsill, looks toward Lena as if startled to find a visitor, then flashes its feathers and flies off.

"As a skate's heel sweeps smooth on a bow-bend: the hurl and gliding / Rebuffed the big wind. My heart in hiding / Stirred for a bird."

Kov turns his head to look at her.

"What's that from?"

"Gerard Manley Hopkins."

He fixes her with his gray-green eyes. There is something in his stare, pity perhaps.

"I'm sorry, Kov. I—I quote from things a lot. I sometimes forget how to talk to people. And quotes help me."

He closes the window and brushes his hands together. "You don't do it to help you talk to people. You do it to preserve your distance."

"Why would I do that?"

"I'm sure you have your reasons."

They move to the round table and sit side by side, looking at the splayed newspaper. She suddenly wonders whether he has that disease, the one where people eat paper or paste. But she knows as well that whatever he is doing is not a disease or an obsession but a rite.

"How's your work?" she asks, touching the corner of the paper.

"I'm trying to repair them," he says. "Some of the files were in binders on those old metal shelves over there." He points. "And, well, you can imagine."

She looks down at the table and has a sudden alarming urge to break off a piece of the paper and put it in her mouth like a communion wafer.

"How do you choose?"

He looks at her with what she supposes would be a questioning look on anyone else, but on him it is more beatific.

"I mean, there are so many," she says. "All the names."

"So many," he agrees. "I do what I can as the morgue keeper."

"Why do you care about the disappeared?"

"I suppose it's about this institution itself."

"The *Record*?"

"The *Record*."

"You're afraid it will disappear?"

"I suppose it seems old-fashioned, but this paper has been my life, and it would be dishonorable to leave it now."

They look down at the paper, as if sitting vigil with a dead friend. Kov picks up a pair of heavy black-handled scissors. "This is how we used to make corrections, by cutting and pasting, literally, cutting with scissors. Quite satisfying."

She leans forward and smooths the paper with her hand. "What did you do here? What was your position?"

"Oh, this and that. Administration."

She picks up the magnifying glass and finds Kov's eyes through the circle. She studies his skin through the glass, a mysterious map. There are roads, but it's hard to tell where they begin, where they lead.

"That's so I can see to clean them. I don't have to read them anymore. I'm just washing the corpse."

"Honoring the dead."

"My son thinks I should be doing other things, but it's important to keep a record."

"Your son?"

Kov doesn't answer but closes his eyes; she does the same. She immediately thinks of Arlene, but she is forgetting her features and instead sees a leg, possibly her own, hoisted over the white rail surrounding the moat around the lions' den. Her legs, then her arms, come into view, the limbs of her younger self. She sees her own bedroom window, where she stands and watches as men disappear into the woods to search for the mountain lion, their flashlights bouncing in the dark like falling stars.

• • •

AS SHE APPROACHES the Recording Room, she sees Russell on his knees, peering through the mail slot.

"Hi, Russell. The handle's still broken."

He jumps up, brushing off his knees. "Sorry. I didn't want to disturb you if you were working."

He follows her inside and she hands him a cassette tape. "I e-mailed the transcript to you."

"That's not why I'm here."

He blushes, a peculiar but not unpleasant tone against his tan skin. He takes a step toward the door and stops, places his hand on top of the overnight machine in a failed effort at nonchalance.

"I'm going to the auditorium for mandatory escape-hood training."

"Oh, right. I'm supposed to be at that. But I have an interview. I wanted to ask you to have a drink tonight, if you don't already have plans."

They agree to meet at the Algonquin at seven thirty.

THE AUDITORIUM IS full and the group is grumpy. Ralph is scheduled to speak, and a group of reporters in the row behind Lena joke about his well-known ad-dresses to the newsroom.

"How long do you think it will take for the first Bear Bryant quote?"

"I'd bet two beers it will be in the first three min—"

Everyone turns to acknowledge Ralph as he walks down the center aisle. His panama hat and gliding gait bring to mind an overseer; Lena watches as he passes her row, half expecting to see him astride a horse and flaunting a riding whip.

He leaps onto the stage, removes his hat, and looks at the crowd with an expression so rigidly serious it seems rehearsed.

"Friends, colleagues, we are gathered here today to issue escape hoods to our valued staff. It is true that our country is at war. And we, the voice of the people, the voice for the people, we are under attack as well. As I'm sure you know, one of our most esteemed colleagues, Katheryn Keel, received personal threats this week, along with an envelope containing white powder that was fortunately found to be flour."

"All-purpose or self-rising?" one of the reporters behind Lena jokes.

"If it was KK's, it had to be self-rising."

"I will not lie, friends," Ralph says, raising his voice. "These are the times that try our souls. But we have it in our power to create the world anew."

"The world anew?" one of the reporters whispers.

"Thomas Paine, I didn't see that one coming. What is he doing, trying to channel Ronald Reagan?"

"What about Yeats? No Yeats?"

" 'The blood-dimmed tide is loosed,' people. Yes, we

have men and women giving their lives every day. But we are under attack, too."

"There's your Yeats. But where's Bear?"

"We are the fourth estate my friends, and though we were not elected, we are the check on all the branches of government. We are the guardian of the guardians, and with this comes the burden of awesome responsibility. When people open their newspapers and read the same article with the same dateline and time stamp that Americans from Peoria to Palmyra are reading, we create among them a sense of imagined community."

"What the hell? Did he get a new speechwriter?"

"And who is it, Peggy Noonan?"

"And, friends, that bond of trust with readers is our most crucial asset, and the preservation of that trust is our most important duty. Information is more than power; it is the reason this irreplaceable newspaper exists. We might be under attack but we will not cower! We will answer our higher calling, we will break with the past, we will forge a new future, and we will continue our reign as the best newspaper on earth because we will overwhelm those hiding information by sheer force! Shock and awe, folks, the Bush administration isn't the only one who can do shock and awe!

"But we want you to be safe. So the *Record* has generously invested in escape hoods to be used in the event of a biological emergency. Now I turn things over to our security consultants, who will instruct you on the proper use of this lifesaving equipment."

Three men onstage explain that they will distribute escape hoods, or SCBAs, self-contained breathing apparatuses ("Or is it apparati?" one asks, ha-ha) to every *Record* employee. The men look like burly flight attendants giving the instructions that will not save a single soul in the event of a real emergency. Those with beards, goatees, and claustrophobia are urged to come forward at the end and "we will help you tighten your hoods." Those allergic to latex are advised not to take one because "we don't know exactly what these are made of." People practice putting them on, and the room takes on the look of a hazmat convention.

As everyone files out of the auditorium clutching their Evolution escape hood boxes, the understanding is that if by chance the hoods are effective, the chosen survivors will not be the meek or the poor, but quick-fingered workers without facial hair or latex allergies.

The reporters who were betting on Ralph's speech are joking about the hoods, but there is anxiety beneath their banter. Lena balances the big orange box as she maneuvers through the hall and thinks of the perverse irony that the terrorist attacks were the *Record*'s last great story, the start of the end of many things. She has come to feel sorry for the haunted-eyed reporters who work harder and longer to chase fragments for their fragmented audience.

An editor claps one of the reporters on the back. "Where's the story on the Islamic principal fired yesterday?"

"I'll have it by five. I just have to—"

"This is the *Record*. If I want yesterday's news tomorrow, I'll go to the *Herald Tribune*."

THE PHONE IS ringing as she pushes the door open and puts down the escape hood. It is a foreign reporter in the field calling because her computer crashed. Lena waits for the call to end, rewinds the tape, and hooks herself to her machine. For the third time in recent days, she feels her body resist.

She takes a deep breath and closes her eyes, blows out through her mouth, trying to empty herself. It is like the dead man's float she learned as a child in the river where she was baptized. You float facedown, the hair fans out around your head, that's called the jellyfish. You have to breathe out slowly so that your body will sink. The water will close over you. You can't see anything even if you open your eyes. Slowly you start to sink. Anyone standing on the shore can't see you. No one would know there's someone sinking to the bottom, the bottom of the world. Once the water closes over you, no one can see.

She stares at the writing on the escape-hood box: "The emergency mask has evolved! One size fits all. And unlike other escape hoods, the Evolution is reusable."

"Reusable?" she says aloud.

"In the event of emergency, simply attach the filter, pull the hood down over your head, and tighten the straps. That's it!"

"That's it!" she says as she lifts the orange hood from the box. It is a strange-smelling material with clear plastic over the eyeholes and a big circle for the filter to fit over the nose and mouth. She puts on her headphones, attaches the filter, and pulls the hood over her head. The familiar emptiness comes over her and she submits, feels herself sinking. She presses the pedal; her fingers pass over the keys.

"A man whose wife, mother, and two sons were killed said comma quote We can see the sea comma but we live in prison comma this life is a prison stop end quote."

Lifting her foot from the pedal, she listens for silence, then the roar on the other side. It passes through her like steel thread. She throws off the hood and walks to the window, leans out toward the pigeon. She leans farther, and the black pavement rises to meet her full on—black! She remembers an article she transcribed—a week ago, a year ago, a thousand years ago?—about a young woman who had jumped from the twenty-third floor of a Midtown high-rise, her brother's apartment. But first, and this was the one detail Lena was certain of, she had taken off her shoes and left them side by side on the balcony. Her hands come into focus; they are white where she is gripping the ledge. She backs away and sinks down against the window.

Inside the room again, she shoves the hood back in its box and tries to stuff it in the trash can, but it won't fit, so she balances it on top. She replaces her headphones, presses the pedal.

"And what about the prospect of this country without civil war question mark this reporter asked the man stop quote It seems as far away comma quote he said comma quote as the clouds in the lofty sky stop end quote."

She looks to her left: the newspaper blurs before her, the letters appear as if under a microscope, little parasites floating on the pulpy page. The news cycle now has no recovery time, we are bombarded with so much news that it has lost its meaning and people look for signposts that they touch like rosaries to order their world, repetition without affect. It did not take long for news of war to be added to the rosary, touched but not felt.

From time to time, she has seen faces on the street and connected them to random stories, but she has never seen the person first, like Arlene, and then recognized that very person, that stranger from the bus, and seen her transformed into print. She had met Arlene and forgotten her; she had read the story and remembered her.

She pushes the revolving doors and leaves the *Record*'s cold air-conditioned lobby for the humid heat of Forty-Third Street. Enclosed briefly in the glass capsule, she daydreams that maybe she will emerge on the other side not only to a different climate but to a different life.

Heat hits her on the other side. Some tourists are posing for pictures under the *Record*'s sign. Midblock, the unmistakable hand reaches from behind its concrete pillar, as if the building itself is demanding a toll. Lena presses a dollar into the open palm. She walks a few feet, then turns back.

"I've been walking by you for years. Will you tell me your name?"

"Guess," the woman says.

"I don't think I can."

"Why not?"

"There are so many names in the world. It's not very likely that I would guess the right one."

"Guess," the woman repeats.

"Mary."

"Ah." She laughs once, short and sharp. "No."

Lena moves closer and looks in the woman's dark eyes. They are a shade of green that reminds her of the colored glass she prized as a child when she made bottle trees.

"I had a name once," the woman says, "but I lost it."

"How did you lose it?"

"I lost everything."

"I bet it's still there, if you want to take it back."

"No," the woman says angrily. "I lost everything. You'd be surprised what you can lose."

"Do you remember where you lost it?"

"No!"

"You could choose a new one."

"No," the woman says. "Really?"

"Why not? What name would you like?"

The woman closes her eyes and tilts her head back, exposing the pale slittable softness of her throat. "Lydia. That was my grandmother's name."

"Good night, Lydia."

"Night, sad-eyed lady."

Lena crosses Times Square, where there is no difference between night and day; the same pedestrians lose speed and equilibrium under the mechanized riptide of tickertape above. How else to explain the sudden jerks, stops, the inability to cross the street, to move out of someone's path, to close an umbrella after the rain has stopped?

THE ALGONQUIN LOBBY is cool and dim. She likes to come here in winter, when she can make a satisfying meal of a book, the free nuts, and a glass of red wine. Russell sits erect in a low, lumpy wing chair.

They order martinis and watch the righteous Algonquin cat sashay through the lobby, eluding outstretched hands.

"I'm so glad this place exists."

"And the cat. She must be twenty years and thirty

pounds by now. What's her name? Mathilde? Mathilde Two?"

The older waiter brings their drinks and places them carefully on cocktail napkins printed with the Dorothy Parker witticism "I love a martini—but two at the most. Three I'm under the table; four, I'm under the host."

The table is low, and the waiter pauses for a painful moment before straightening with a tight smile, one hand on his lower back.

"Enjoy."

"Cheers," Russell says.

She sips the clear flame slowly, welcoming the burn in her throat. She takes the folded newspaper clipping from her pocket and places it on her knee.

"What's that?"

She passes the warm piece of paper to him, the most intimate gesture she has made in a long time.

"Her again. You're obsessed, aren't you?"

"I know you said that never happens to you, but why not? Isn't there ever a story you work on that you can't let go?"

"Not really."

She takes a bigger sip of the drink, the taste a little subtler now. A couple sits uncomfortably together on a nearby couch. The man looks unhappily at the woman, who shifts on the flattened cushion. He swirls his drink aggressively and looks at his wife. She has beautiful, sensible silver hair and sturdy shoes.

"Are you ready to leave?" she asks.

"No."

The woman looks down at her chenille jumper, which has served her well in some small academic town, and seems to realize that she does not travel as well as her wrinkle-resistant fabric. Her husband seems to say with each swirl of his drink that he realized this long ago. He can take her places, but she won't travel.

Lena balances the drink on her crossed leg, and Russell reaches out, touching her knee.

"Is this where you brought her?" the woman on the couch asks.

The husband looks at her and frowns, throwing his swizzle stick like a spear in his drink. "Margaret, it was a crime of opportunity."

"That's funny," the woman says bitterly. "That's the funniest thing you've said in years."

"Crimes of opportunity," Lena says, sliding the martini's olive in her mouth.

They follow the cat's indifferent gaze to watch the couple leave. The husband throws out his unfaithful arms, gesturing for his wife to proceed.

"Russell, doesn't it seem strange that someone could just disappear?"

"People are pretty easy to find," he says, "except when no one bothers to look. It's almost impossible not to leave some kind of record—technology is too sophisticated. There are so many ways a person can be tracked. Also, the brutal truth is that she was an unknown woman, a dead woman. It's hard enough to interest readers in missing unknowns, but dead unknowns, that's a story with no future."

Lena looks down at the clipping that Russell has put on the table between them, the colorless photo static and unrevealing.

"I read recently that the average American lives about a thousand months. How many newspapers would that be?"

"One thousand times, well, approximately thirty, so thirty thousand."

"Thirty thousand newspapers equal a life."

"In a sense."

"A record."

"Well, a record of the days, not of the life."

"Precisely."

"Lena, are you OK?"

"I just feel that Arlene has been abandoned. No obit, no follow-up, just perished, printed, recycled."

"Lena, the story's dead. Arlene's dead. There's nothing else to say."

"But how do you reconcile things?"

"What things?"

"The news, life—observing, recording, living."

"Reporters aren't moralists. We're guardians."

"Guardians of what?"

"Not what we used to be. Now we're just trying to keep up."

"Do you ever feel that living the news, breathing it, day after day, that it harms your . . ."

"My what?"

"Soul."

"We try to stay objective. And our souls are full of ink."

She looks at the couch where the couple was sitting. "That couple that just left, did you hear them?"

"No, I wasn't listening."

"I was. What if I really am turning into a tape recorder? It's frightening."

Russell looks at her with a pleasantly bland and relaxed, almost dreamy, expression he acquires when he is interviewing. Lena has wondered whether he has had Botox, but now she thinks he has retained the unlined look of youth without medical help.

"I'm going to kiss you now," he says, taking her by surprise. He grips her shoulders and draws her to him and kisses her slowly, with a skill and confidence that contrasts with his slightly awkward ways.

Outside, he hails a cab and places a hand on her lower back as he opens the door for her. Their heads knock together as she leans forward to adjust her skirt and he leans toward her, closing the door behind him. They share a thirty-block kiss, pause while he pays the driver, and then pick up again as they climb the stairs to his apartment.

His shoes are lined up outside the door.

"Shoes aren't allowed inside?"

"No." He kicks off his loafers and bends down to unbuckle her sandals.

"I'll do it—"

"No, let me."

She looks down at the back of his boyish head as he kneels to gently remove her shoes.

He leads her inside the apartment, which has more charm than she would have expected, the small, slightly messy abode of someone who has a life both inside and outside the home.

"Does the fireplace work?"

"No."

He opens a bottle of wine and she examines his bookshelves. There's a book about the terrorist attack written by two *Record* reporters. She takes it down and rubs the cover without opening it. She transcribed more than 250,000 words for this book, which she has not read, though she keeps the copy the reporters gave her. She knows what's inside, if not the particular arrangement. The acknowledgments thank her among many others, an unexpected gesture that touched her.

She replaces the book as Russell returns with red wine, which he hands to her, kissing her nose. She doesn't know whether it is too soon to tell him she hates being kissed on the nose, so she smiles and sticks her nose in the glass.

"It's nothing special," he says.

"My favorite kind."

He takes off his glasses, and his eyes are like the eyes of an animal coming out of hibernation. She has the same feeling: her whole body is like that, coming awake, shaking off the lethargy.

"You said you were leaving on assignment tomorrow. Where are you going?"

"To Washington. Soldiers' bodies are arriving from Baghdad, from Germany really—they're flown from Iraq to Germany to Fort Dix to Washington. We're doing a story on how the administration won't let their coffins be photographed."

She remembers a photo that had sparked some conversation and then disappeared. It was of an airplane at an airport gate. In the photo, a few passengers were peering out their porthole windows. Below, in the plane's belly, flag-draped coffins were being prepared for unloading. The passengers above could not see and still had no idea that death had been onboard.

"They don't want people to see the war."

"Or dead people."

"It's strange how they put so much effort into creating

a war and convincing people to go along with it and now they want people to forget we're in it."

"And they've been effective at both."

"Invisible bodies," she says. "They're all around us, aren't they?"

He takes her glass and puts it down on the table. "You're not invisible, even if you try to be. I've been wondering." He kisses her.

She tries to concentrate on kissing him back and ignores the familiar feeling that her body is vaporizing. He takes her hand and leads her into the bedroom, and she follows him eagerly because she wants to feel hands on her skin and the heaviness of her limbs.

The sex is sweet, fumbling, better than she would have guessed. They draw back and smile at each other, surprised at their passion, or at least their enthusiasm. Sleep comes slowly for her and fast for him, but in the morning when she blinks awake, Russell is showered and stands near the bed, buttoning up his button-down. She blinks again, not quite believing that she slept while he was awake, up, moving around and preparing for the day.

He sits on the bed. "Don't get up, it's early. I have to catch the shuttle."

She struggles up on her elbows. "I'll be quick."

"No, it's early. I want you to stay. Take your time, there's coffee in the kitchen. The door will lock behind you." He kisses her forehead. "I like to think of you here."

She looks down and leans into him as he strokes her hair, remembering the image of the zoo sea lions bumping against the glass.

"Stay."

She nods.

When he leaves, she spreads her arms and legs in the bed. It is a midwestern bed, soft, beige, and unfairly spacious. She rolls over and stretches out her arms, which still don't touch the edge. She had underestimated the impact of a big, comfortable bed in her life.

In the kitchen she pours a cup of coffee that Russell has left warming in the pot. The silence of the apartment is different from the silence of her room, and she wanders freely, pausing to pull the same book from the bookshelf in the living room. It's hefty in her hand, but not as heavy as it would be if all the quarter of a million words she transcribed were included. She remembers only a few of the interviews and only one with any clarity. It was a security guard who had been at the front desk greeting people, "all my happy faces, all my people." Looking unseeingly at the text, she hears his voice, clear and distinct. "That particular morning it struck me that the foot traffic was lighter, and it wasn't until later I realized that it was Election Day.

"And I'm just standing there wondering where everyone is when I hear this tremendous roar. I thought, It's probably nothing. But then it came back and started getting louder and louder. I looked to my left and that's when I saw this tremendous fireball roaring out of the lobby of building number one. And it appeared that it was pushing hundreds of people in front of it.

"This is where my memory fades out. I remember running. Then I blacked out and came to in silence and darkness. And around the same time I caught through my left eye, in the periphery, coming toward me, two figures. And they were fully engulfed. They were running toward me. They ran past me. And it was silent."

She closes the book and turns it over to the back cover, where two reporters look out with placid credibility. Let us sort it out for you, they seem to say. Let us cut it down and put it between the covers of a book so that it's bite-size, ingestible, digestible. It's not their fault, Lena says to herself, that the massive amount of information, and the continual cycle of commentary, has blunted all meaning.

She glances at the chapter headings, flips through the pages. It starts with the story of the architect. The man who built the then-tallest buildings in the world had a fear of heights. Was that prophetic? The acrophobic architect, the fine fault line between attraction and repulsion, is something she understands. She puts the book back on the shelf and stares at the row of spines. For the first time, she thinks of bookshelves as plots in a vast potter's field, except these dead can be claimed and known each time someone selects them from the shelf.

She continues to wander, making the bed, brushing her teeth with her index finger, rinsing her coffee cup. Looking for Russell's cup to rinse, she realizes that he didn't drink any coffee: he made it for her.

On his clunky schoolboy desk are stacks of tan reporter's notebooks, like sandbags against a sea of uncertainty. Looking closer, she sees that they are dated and arranged by year. The top one on the nearest stack is from this month; the pages are full of scribbles and the last entry is less than a week old. It is not hard to find the entry on Arlene. In Russell's small but legible script there is a number for Mount Sinai, the name of the spokesman, Fred Klamm, and two phone numbers, one crossed out. "Confirmed that A. Lebow admitted on July 8," he has written, "body sent to the hosp. morgue, then to city morgue (Bellevue)."

Klamm quote: "Take very seriously, blah, blah, blah, quotes on tape."

At the bottom of the page, he has scrawled, "Follow-up? A. Lebow's address, 317 Ave. C (Stuy Town), Apt. 3B."

She writes down the address and puts the notebook back on top of the stack. As she leaves, she takes one last look around, then closes the door and turns the knob to make sure all is safely locked inside.

CHAPTER NINE

Break-in at Dead Woman's Apartment; Scientists Date Van Gogh's Moonrise

She does not have to wait long outside Arlene's Stuyvesant Town building. A woman pushing a stroller struggles with the door, and Lena holds it open, then follows her inside. The woman pushes the stroller toward the elevator, so Lena enters the stairwell, which is wide and industrial. The concrete walls and iron rails make it seem more like a school than an apartment building.

On the third floor, she knocks softly on Arlene's door. There is no answer, and almost as a reflex she tries the doorknob. It's unlocked. She opens the door and puts her head inside.

"Hello?"

At the sound of a child's voice from somewhere down the hall, she steps inside and closes the door as quietly as possible.

So this is the Stuy Town appeal: by Manhattan standards, it's huge. A cleaning crew must have left the door unlocked. The harsh scent of fake pine fills the room. Empty boxes are stacked along the walls, waiting for the dead tenant's belongings. The parquet floors are uncarpeted and she tiptoes into the central room even though she is wearing soft-soled espadrilles. Somehow it feels like the living space of a quiet person. She lifts her arms up to shoulder height and lets them fall; so much space in the middle of Manhattan is hard to comprehend. No one would stumble over anything here, she thinks, not even a blind person. Maybe Arlene liked the spaciousness, maybe she could close the door and live privately, expansively. This space of her own allowed her a private life, something not allowed for animals at the zoo.

The small, old-fashioned kitchen is tidy and bright, with a white gas stove, white cupboards, and a small green refrigerator, butter and carrots and cereal the only things inside it. Cereal in the fridge—that's something that Lena always did when she had a kitchen. It is something she never thought much about, but roommates and friends seemed to find if very strange. She wonders whether Arlene had to explain this to people, too, and whether she told them, as Lena did, that she didn't want to attract mice, when really she just liked to keep her cereal cold.

She carries the box of cereal into the living room, where a built-in bookshelf runs the entire length of the wall. She takes a few books from the shelves, runs her fingers over the letters, but they remain dead to her, unable to be raised.

She grabs a handful of cereal and munches as she walks down the hall, holding the box to her chest. There is no answer when she knocks on the closed bedroom door. She listens carefully, with her transcriptionist's ears, but she cannot hear a sound except for a protest from her throat for swallowing dry cereal. With her eyes closed, she turns the knob and gently pushes the door open. A puff of air hits her face, blowing a strand of hair in her eyes, which have fluttered open and blinked against the breeze that is coming in from the open window, lifting the white curtains. The room is spare, the unadorned space of a monk or a scholar, with a double bed, a dresser, a bedside table stacked with four books in braille.

She pauses at the closed closet door. Until now the invasion of privacy has been excusable, if only in her own mind, because she will leave things exactly as she found them, as if they have not been touched. But the closet is different. She stands in front of it, trying to decide whether to open it.

A noise from the window causes her to turn around. Parting the curtains, she sees a dirt dauber fly against the glass before crashing down to the sill. He does this again and again, and at first she does not know how to respond. The windows crank open and shut; there are no screens. Guiding him with her hand does not seem to help. Finally, when she thinks he will bash his dirt dauber brains out, she grabs him between her fingers and flings him outside.

She did not know dirt daubers lived in the North; she always associated their heavy slowness with the South. She tries to remember the last time she saw one. Sinking down to kneel beside the window, she parts the white curtains and tucks them behind her ears like hair, as she used to do in her bedroom, where she would watch from the window as her father walked up and down the rows of the field, "inspecting" them, as her mother had called it. And after she died, he inspected them even more. Her father preached shared suffering but he grieved in his solitude, as did she. At home, nothing was shared, suffering least of all.

The dirt road ran beside the field; many nights it was illuminated by the moonlight's white fire, and she would watch for him, the mountain lion, as her father's feet thudded softly through the thick dirt, rising and falling between the rows of seedlings, from which all he asked was silence. He was too modest to ask for their obedience, or even to pray for it.

Sometimes, if she watched long enough, she would see a shadow move on the road near the ditch. And she would press her face against the screen and strain to see the body she had heard described as a supple, overgrown cat, tawny and long tailed, with binocular vision and a legendary scream.

A movement in the courtyard catches her eye; a man is walking a Labrador retriever. They shamble along with the same heavy-hipped gait. She moves away from the window, sits down on the double bed. She looks down at her legs; her linen pants are beginning to wrinkle, and she feels her body relax into the mattress that once held Arlene's weight but never will again. As she runs her hands over the white embroidered bedspread, a weariness washes over her, and she lies down in the dimness. Laying her head against the indented pillow, she wonders whether it cradled Arlene's head in the same perfectly contouring way. She turns her head toward the window, and her cheek brushes against the pillowcase, which gives off the scent of lavender and bananas that she has smelled in Kov's room. Her hands relax against the spread and she closes her eyes.

In the dream it is always summer. There is only the sun, the road, and the two of them.

"Arlene?"

She does not turn back. The road runs before them and behind them, unbroken in either direction like a barren and elongated row of the field where no crops grow.

"Arlene."

Then she begins to run.

"You. Listen!"

And she begins to run behind her, though she is terrified to see her face. They run, the air filled with the metallic smell of insects singed by the sun. You forget how big they can be until you crash into them on summer nights. She runs faster, she can hear Arlene's breath now; they are younger, then older, then younger again as they run, burning through the days. The distance is not far and she lifts her hand—

"Arlene!"

There is no one else. She is closer and can hear Arlene's breath and her own breath and the road—

Suddenly he passes them—first her, then Arlene. He passes them without a sound, the riven, fur-coated skin flowing from his back like Joseph's cape. The cat's movement is smooth, unbroken, his mutilated beauty is almost unbearable.

The hunters, she thinks, they have finally got him. But

just as she thinks it, he is somehow beside her again, and he turns his masklike face to her, and as their eyes meet, the shock of recognition makes her cry out.

They continue to run. They are engulfed, running and burning, all silence now, and in the dream she understands that they will run forever and she will never reach them and the road will never end.

Her own moaning awakens her and she quickly straightens the bed and rushes from the room.

Passing again through the front room, she pauses at a round table near the bookshelves. There is a computer and, beside it, a cassette player with a set of headphones. She does not even think of privacy or violation; she is not thinking at all when she sits down before the computer and slips on the headphones. It is muscle memory that allows her to rewind the tape as she wonders if words will sound different through Arlene's headset. Suddenly, Arlene's voice is in her ear: "This is my last entry. I am through with this body. It is my choice. I want to inhabit the lion's body. It is not that I think I will become the lion. I am not crazy. I don't want to disappear, to fade. But I wish to be devoured, devoured by something that does not speak. Not in our language anyway.

"Maybe we are as we move through the world. If I cannot inhabit the lion's body, then at least I can be a small part of him as he moves through the world. I hope that for a moment as he devours my body the lion will be satisfied, that it will remind him of his wildness of spirit, that it will remind him that he is a lion."

ALONE IN HER room at Parkside, Lena yanks the string above the sink and the light buzzes on. There is something painful about living in a room with a sink, though it is difficult to say what it is. The gray-green carpet underneath sometimes gets damp and it feels awful underfoot. Or maybe it is that lying in bed, she can see the sink's naked udder leading to exposed pipes. But she cannot consider a sink skirt either. That would be worse. Hardware should not wear costumes. Of that, at least, she is certain.

"The one certainty of my future," she says to herself in the mirror. "No tea cozies, no toilet fuzzies, no toaster covers, no sink skirts, no Kleenex cases."

She looks at herself in the medicine cabinet mirror, turns her head to the right, the left. She overheard a former boyfriend describe her once as "attractive, un-aggressively so." She examines herself, wondering what remains. Hazel eyes, faded red hair, unremarkable features, good teeth. She parts her lips and examines her inheritance, white and serviceable. As she turns her head slowly from side to side, the black spot appears in the corner of her left eye. She watches it spread, signaling the static vision that comes with migraines. But she doesn't

have a migraine; she hasn't had one since the day she saw
Arlene. She lifts her hand and waves it slowly before her
eyes. It is like a dismembered hand, a ghost of her own,
and she remembers an experiment from one of her college seminars where students lifted their hands quickly
when the lights were flashed, and then they sat in the
dark, all seeing the white ghost of their own hands float
before them. Persistence of memory, the professor had
called it.

She jumps when the phone rings, so seldom does it
ring, and so late.

"It's after midnight. Do you know what today is?"

"Hi, Russell. Today, July thirteenth?"

"It's the date Van Gogh saw the moon in Saint-Rémy,
the one he painted in *Moonrise*."

"How do you know?"

"Scientists took elevation readings and measurements.
Isn't that amazing? They took a painting over a century old
and were able to calculate that the moonrise depicted for
eternity occurred on July thirteenth, 1889, at 9:08 p.m."

"Is that what intrigues you, the destruction of mystery?"

"The solving of mystery. That's why I'm a reporter."

"To solve mysteries? I thought you were spreaders of
information, recorders of fact."

"Yeah, that, too. So, what's it like in there?"

"It's tiny, quiet, not so bad. Do you think it's strange
that I live here?"

CHAPTER TEN

Lion That Mauled
Woman in Limbo

The next day she calls in sick, rents a car, and drives 120 miles north of the city to the Cullen Animal Sanctuary. It is on sixty acres abutting the Hudson River; she has to look closely for the small roadside sign at the end of the long, unpaved driveway.

A single chain blocks the winding drive, so she parks the car and walks up the path. Trees and vegetation are thick on either side, obscuring the sanctuary grounds. She goes only a little way before a pickup truck approaches from ahead and a woman with clipped, curly hair leans out of the driver's side window.

"Are you the one who called from the *Record*?"

"Right. Lena Respass."

"Hop in."

The woman is stocky and strong and completely at ease behind the wheel of the pickup, though she is so short that she sits forward to drive. She introduces herself as Jackie Wade, and Lena is grateful that she does not say much as they turn around and speed up the driveway, which is nearly a half mile long and lined with thick-limbed trees whose leaves flash silvery undersides as they pass. At one point Lena instinctively ducks as a low-hanging oak branch swipes the truck's windshield.

"We should cut those back," Jackie says, "but there's never time."

When they round the final curve, the sanctuary is exposed. Stables and outbuildings fan out behind a two-story farmhouse, painted white with a red tin roof. A sloping lawn fronts the house, and a grazing goat pauses to lift its head and stare in the truck's direction.

"That's Billie. We reward his orneriness by letting him roam. He enjoys mowing the grass at least."

"How many animals do you have?"

"We're small, fiftysome, not counting the dogs and cats. We have three llamas, two bears, a few monkeys, horses, parrots, an ostrich, lambs, and turkeys. We had a marmoset until yesterday. Robert is our only lion. He's in limbo right now, but he'll go to a wild game sanctuary in California when he's recovered enough."

"What happened to the marmoset?"

"We think it was a heart attack. We tried to give him mouth-to-mouth, but we couldn't revive him."

She stops the truck in front of the farmhouse and turns to Lena. Even in repose she seems a bustling, good-natured woman, one who lives by physical labor. A solid woman.

"Do you name them all?"

"What, the animals? Yes. Some of them come with names, and others we call whatever seems to suit them." She corrects herself. "Whatever seems to suit *us*. I am not silly enough to try to humanize them, but when you live with this many animals it makes sense to call them something."

They sit for a minute, assessing each other in the enclosed cab of the truck. Lena feels like one of the lost animals seeking refuge as Jackie looks at her with appraising eyes that hold neither coldness nor sentimentality. It is the first time in years Lena has missed the plainspoken farmers she grew up with, people who would not waste time debating things neither of you were ever going to agree on, but who even so would be the first to come to your aid if you needed help. People who looked at you and knew who you were.

"Would you like to go inside and talk or do you want to see Robert first?"

"I want to see him," Lena says, unable to call him by the ridiculous name.

Jackie leads her around the back of the farmhouse, past a wide dirt patch where hay bales are scattered. "We have a trainer who comes in to take him to the fenced-in area where he has room to run, but Robert prefers to stay in the cage. It is hard to coax him out, and we have tried just about everything. He's suffered a shock; it will take time."

A chestnut tree shades the cage, and sunlight and shadow dapple his blond body. He lies in complete stillness, his head erect, the stance of a sphinx, a breathing statue.

"Robert, you have a visitor. Someone came to see you."

The lion remains utterly still in his majestic indifference. Lena sits down on a hay bale in front of the cage and looks at him through the bars.

"Is he eating?"

"Not much, but we're working on it. He is hesitant with food, but eventually we'll find something he has a taste for."

A tall, paunchy man with a red face and a feed-and-seed store cap walks toward them with a stiff-legged gait.

"My husband, Bill," Jackie says in brief introduction.

With a glance, he dismisses Lena as a Manhattan media person who has no place in this rural realm.

"The vet called, Jackie. He wants you to reconsider Prozac."

"I don't want to do it," she says, shaking her head and rubbing her right hand where a scratch has puckered the skin.

"I don't either, Jackie, hell, I wouldn't take it and I wouldn't want you to. But they have these drugs now, I don't know, Tom says it may help him transition to his new setting. He's been through a lot."

"Transition?" Jackie says. "Listen to you. Of course he's been through a lot, but will drugging him help? How would he tell us? He's depressed now, we can see that. And when he is content we will see that, too."

"I told him you'd call him back. Can we discuss this inside?"

"You'll be all right here for a while?" Jackie asks Lena, who nods, eager to be alone with the lion.

She watches them walk toward the house, him stiff and upright, her solid and flat footed, with the walk of a farmer's wife. Turning back toward the cage, Lena bends forward, hands on knees, and stares at him. His eyes do not blink; his gaze does not stray. She thinks she sees one ear twitch but then cannot be sure. A fly explores the wide, flat nose one nostril at a time and is acquiesced to without a movement. She is transfixed by the lion's immobility.

"I thought it would get easier. You, too? Did you think life in the cage would get easier? That's not what happens, is it?"

She drags a hay bale closer and sits down again; he has not flinched. "Let me look at you," she says, as if asking permission. Leaning closer, she examines the lion's pinhead-size pupils. It is as if everything lies behind this leonine mask, the pupils a point of entry to a place she must know. But even as this occurs to her in a wordless thought, she sees that access will be denied, not by his will but simply because the gap is unbreachable. She sits back.

"You did as she asked. You escorted her to death. Not that that's your trouble. Is it that you remembered what life could be, or your mind was confused by your muscle's memory? Have we committed the crime of making you an in-between, no longer lion, unable to be anything else? Are we both in-betweens?"

She leans forward, her face close to the cage, and looks into his golden-green eyes. "If a lion could speak, we wouldn't understand it." The lion yawns, revealing the inside of his enormous mouth, pink and vulnerable as a shelled mollusk. "What? You've heard that one before?"

But he will not be moved by a human voice; it evokes nothing in him and offers nothing for him. As she stands to go, shame comes over her with a completeness that sends her to her knees in surprise. And even as she observes herself there on the ground in front of the lion, she cannot help her physical reaction to this creature of impotent power.

She has an urge to flee, but as she gets up and approaches the house, Jackie opens the door and ushers her inside. The sunny white kitchen is small but uncluttered; there are no ornaments or knickknacks or craftsy items except for a wall clock in the shape of a birdhouse.

They sit at a table covered with a plastic blue-and-white-checkered tablecloth, drinking bitter coffee. Lena has trouble listening as Jackie tells her about the workings of the sanctuary. After a brief attempt to take notes in her reporter's notebook, snagged from the Recording Room supply closet, she says she doesn't feel well and asks if they can continue another time.

DRIVING BACK TO the city, she has to pull over on the side of the road. It is not as if she has ever taken much interest in animal welfare. Growing up on a farm, she accepted the hierarchy of life and the randomness of death.

The tears start with a trickle, then flow faster, so that she could not wipe them away even if she tried. As she looks through the windshield at the green countryside, the memory comes to her, stark and undeniable. She is in the truck with her father; the sun is setting behind the trees, turning the pine treetops into a ring of bloody fur on the horizon. They drive toward it, not seeming to get closer, as if the trees are hiding something. A group of men stand on the shoulder of the road, looking down at the ground. Her father brakes, and one of the men, Lynzie, comes to the open driver's window.

"We got him."

"Who?"

"The mountain cat. William Boyd hit him with his twenty-two. You want to see him?"

"No, Dad, no."

He looked over at her but responded only to Lynzie. "We better get back. Margaret's home by herself."

As Lena and her father drove past, one of the men reached out and nudged the cat with his foot, then said something that caused the group to laugh together as one. She didn't know the shooter but she could tell which one he was because he laughed and blushed and patted his face as the other men slapped him on the shoulder. She looked, she couldn't help it, and there he was, so much smaller than she imagined, just a big-pawed, overgrown cat with his long, now-useless tail sticking straight out behind him. His face seemed too small for his body, and his eyes were open, a look in them as if to say, What have you done to me? What have you done?

CHAPTER ELEVEN

Baby Pulled from
Earthquake Rubble

In the morning, the light is flashing on the overnight machine when she opens the Recording Room door. She switches on the lights, presses "play."

"Hi. This is Russell, calling for the transcriptionist. Slug it Seduction; dateline: Eros, July fifteenth; desk: personal; editor: unnecessary."

She laughs and raises the volume on the machine.

"Lead: A mysterious auburn-haired woman has been observed for quite some time in a drab building in Midtown stop. She is believed to be the last newspaper transcriptionist in America stop. Her habits are hard to discern but she is fond of quoting dead people and has been known to talk to pigeons stop. She has a soft spot for the disappeared and comma one hopes comma near-sighted metro reporters who carry red backpacks and still rely on cassette tapes and pencils stop. Correction: please make that Ebony 6325 pencils stop.

"Adds to follow. Note to transcriptionist: This reporter will be unavailable for a day or so while he works on a story in DC. But he will be happy to hear the transcriptionist's reaction to his dictation upon return. Also, sensitive passages of this ongoing story have been redacted to protect the guilty and for job security purposes, but we could review them in person. Bye for now, Lena."

She saves the message and thinks of transferring it to tape and recording a message for Russell, but the phone rings. A baby has been found after an earthquake in South Asia that has left many dead or missing.

"No one can remember who brought the baby to the hospital and it was not recorded because of the chaotic scramble to save the living stop. But baby number sixty-seven comma so named because he was the sixty-seventh patient admitted after the quake comma has so far been claimed by seven couples stop."

She yanks on the cord from the headphones. She pumps the foot pedal but cannot get comfortable and strains against her electrical tether.

"There has been so much interest in the baby that hospital staff members have been hiding him in the operating room at night out of fear that he might be kidnapped stop.

"One woman claimed she recognized the shape of his mouth stop. When asked if she would submit to DNA tests she said comma quote They can cut out my tongue and test it if they need to stop.

"Quote I know he is mine stop. I know he is my son stop end quote."

As she is standing by the recording phones rewinding the tape and thinking of the lost child being hidden in the operating room like Moses in the bushes, the unbearable urge to flee overwhelms her. She takes the phones off the hooks. One day this is going to catch up with me, she thinks, as she writes "Be back in 10 minutes" and the time and presses the Post-it note on the door.

The cafeteria has metal turnstiles—like courthouses and amusement parks—so that employees cannot escape without paying, which would seem to contradict the *Record*'s touted belief in trust and the honor system. It is a long room with big windows overlooking Forty-Third Street and, in the distance, Times Square. It is only the twelfth floor, but it seems higher, a sort of limbo where lost and empty plastic bird-bags float through the steam from the Cup Noodles billboard outside the window. Plastic plants hang in the cafeteria windows like strange seaweed monsters that chase children down the beach in a Fellini version of childhood; long plastic tendrils drape the heads of those who sit too close. There are plain tables and brownish plastic chairs, and on the walls are pictures colored by schoolchildren. It could be the cafeteria of a middle school or an insane asylum.

This is not the executive dining room, which lies at the end of the carpeted hallway lined with pictures of all of the *Record*'s Pulitzer Prize winners. Lena has never been inside the executive dining room, which is attended by uniformed wait staff. She has been down the hall under the pretext of studying the Pulitzer portraits, but her real purpose was to swipe one of the chocolate mints kept in a candy dish near the dining room door.

In line at the cash register, a fat pinkish manager in a buttoned polo shirt tries to speak to Joe, the cashier, in Spanish. Joe nods sympathetically, as he is Taiwanese.

"You have met my friend?" Joe asks when she pays for the coffees.

"Him?" she asks, nodding toward the manager.

"No, my friend, birdman."

"You know Kov?"

"We watch for each other. We know everybody. You day people have the day world, but the cleaners, the cafeteria, the workers, we have the night. Other world. Birdman is good man. He tells me how to train my racing pigeons. You know who he is?"

"What do you mean?"

"Pop."

She assumes Joe means this as a sign of respect, so she doesn't tell him that Pop might not be a welcome nickname.

"Why do you call him that?"

"Because he comes first. He is an important man."

"Yes, he is."

ON THE FIFTH floor, she walks down the empty hall to the blue door. After looking both ways, then down at the coffee cups in either hand, she tilts her head toward the door. "Kov, it's me, Lena." No answer. "Now the day is over," she sings softly. "Night is drawing nigh."

Silence. But not complete silence; the lights buzz overhead, a strange kind of music. And from the other side of the door comes the unmistakable voice: "Shadows of the evening steal across the sky."

Kov opens the door and sweeps his arm in a shallow arc of welcome. He leads her to the circular table, where a newspaper is spread open to the obituaries, a bloodless autopsy.

"I thought you might like some coffee. I mean, if you like coffee. I hope I'm not interrupting."

"Interruptions remind us we want to return to what we were doing, that it is worthwhile. Please, sit down and join me."

She puts the coffee cups on the table. "I don't know how you take it."

"However it comes."

"Black."

"Good."

He pulls a chair out for her nimbly, without making a sound. She wonders whether noiselessness is something he has learned from necessity, but suspects it is something he has always known.

"Kov?" She starts to ask him about the pigeon X-ray but can't. They sit and sip their coffee, the newspaper between them on the table.

ITALO CALVINO, ITALIAN FABULIST, DEAD AT 61 is the headline of the September 20, 1985, obituary.

"It is not the voice that commands the story: it is the ear," she says, quoting the dead man on the table.

They look down in silence, paying their respects to the author of *Invisible Cities*.

"So, I went to see her, Arlene's sister, Ellen Lebow. She's a Chaucer scholar." She doesn't say anything about her visit to the lion. It is too painful to share.

Kov does not respond; instead he reaches for a stack of papers on the table. The page on top has a series of labeled numbers—permit number, section number, plot number, grave number, age of deceased, date permit was issued, date of death, cause of death.

"What's this?"

"I've been thinking. If no one is sure where Arlene is buried, but it's most likely that she's in the potter's field on Hart Island, then a determined person ought to be able to find her."

"How?"

"They keep burial records."

"But Russell said they told him they couldn't find Arlene's name on the log."

"Well, it wouldn't hurt to go out there and have a look around."

"But it's closed to the public, I checked. You have to have permission from the Corrections Department."

"I made a phone call. There's a burial detail taking the ferry from City Island this afternoon. I've arranged for you to go as a sort of honorary observer, if you wish."

"But how?"

"It's the morgue keepers network; I called an old friend. I've been here a long time, Lena. I'm a part of this institution. Sometimes that can help, if you let it."

She stares at the xeroxed stack of pages, thin as shaved bone.

"I don't understand."

"These are photocopies of old records. They keep entries for each body buried on Hart Island. Bellevue's records might be incomplete, but the cemetery has its own records. This is a photocopy of an old record book—section, plot, grave."

"Why are you helping me, Kov?"

"You and I are both part of the *Record*'s institutional memory. Howard is letting go of that," he says, surprising her by speaking of the publisher so informally. "He's letting some things slip from sight with the transformation. And technology is tremendously useful, but it is also fragile."

"How do you know Howard?"

"I've been here a long time, Lena. Howard and I, as they say, go way back."

CHAPTER TWELVE

Finding the Forgotten on Hart Island

When she arrives at the City Island dock, the corrections officer confirms that she is on "the list" and waves her onto the ferry with the Corrections Department van, the prison bus, and the morgue truck. The ride across Long Island Sound to Hart Island is quick but not quiet. The prisoners are visibly, physically relieved to be outside, and even though they wear shackles on the ferry, they know they will be unbound on the other side.

One of the corrections officers has opened the doors and windows of the bus, and the prisoners' voices overlap with the gulls' cries overhead.

"Across the River Styx and we'll be free," one of them says.

"For a while," another says.

"Don't ruin it for him. We'll be outside, we'll be movin' and sweatin' and lookin' at the sky. Can't even see the prison from there, can't see those bars at all."

"What are we doin' out here anyway? Gardening?"

"Yeah," someone says, "we're returning things to the soil. Dust to dust, and all that."

"You mean you don't know what you signed up for, man?" says another.

"The warden just said outside work, heavy lifting."

"Yeah, but you mean you don't know?"

"Know what?"

"We out here to bury people, man, to bury people that nobody claimed and don't nobody want. We gonna stack 'em up and cover 'em over. It's Hart Island, that's where they bury dead people whose folks don't want them. That's what we're here to do."

"You shittin' me?"

"We're the burial detail. It ain't so bad, I just hope there's no babies today. That's cold work even in the heat of day. Itty-bitty pine boxes, hundreds in a row."

"From Rikers Island to Hart Island, that's cold," someone says, and the bus goes quiet.

The boat bumps against the dock and comes to a stop. The morgue truck is first off, followed by the prison bus and the van. The caravan drives slowly past the ferry slip, where a new-looking PRISON, KEEP OFF sign is posted on an old blue structure reminiscent of a county fair ticket booth.

They drive along the dirt road, past the empty buildings of the former boys' reformatory. The old brick buildings, the brownish red of dried blood, make the island seem even emptier than if it were barren and unbroken. The windowless window frames and doorless entrances reveal glimpses of the dark inside. One of the buildings has a sign that says BUTCHER SHOP on white board above the entrance.

It is a bright, hot day and the prevailing sound when they turn toward Cemetery Hill is the song of unseen insects. The vehicles stop before a freshly dug trench; mussel shells and a retaining wall partially cover a few rows of raw pine boxes.

The inmates spill out of the bus, blinking against the sun. They stand patiently as three men in uniform move among them, unlocking the shackles. One man, the one they call "Captain," stands nearby watching, his hands on his holster.

"Aaahhhh," one man says. He moves his wrists, then leans down, touches his toes, and does a jumping jack.

"Careful," one of the officers says. "Not too quick."

The driver of the morgue truck opens the door to the truck bed.

"How many we got today?"

"Eleven."

"I want two in the truck to pass the box, two behind the truck to unload, two by the trench to pass them down, and two in the trench to stack and pack."

The inmates are quiet; one looks up at the sky as if to consider whether the price to be paid for time outside is worth it. Another, who has walked around to the back of the truck, suddenly covers his mouth and nose.

"Oh, oh. They stink."

"So would you if somebody left your forgotten ass to rot in a hot box till some convict could put you in a hole."

"Oh, shit, man, how long they been in there?"

"It's summer, what do you expect? Some have been in there longer than others. We've got to have enough to make a trip out here. Also, we've got to work with your schedules. They keep you busy in prison with all your activities."

An older prisoner puts his hand on the shoulder of the one who still covers his mouth. "First time is the hardest. Stand there by the trench, you just pass 'em down and enjoy the sunshine on your face and be glad you can breathe out in open air."

The prisoner nods, looking down at the ground, and goes to stand by the trench.

They pair up without another word and begin their work. In their dark jumpsuits and white cotton gloves, they look like pantomimists performing a timeless dance, both ancient and modern.

"You sure you're a reporter?" the captain asks Lena.

Startled, she turns toward him. "What do you mean?"

"You're too quiet. You've hardly said a word. I've seen a lot of things, but I've never seen a quiet reporter."

"It seems like a quiet place," she says. "It seems like a place to be quiet."

"True enough. But you know what they say: you have to watch out for the quiet ones."

"So they say."

The prisoners work with smooth movements. The bare boxes are slid along the truck bed by white gloves attached to unseen bodies, handed down to those waiting below, passed to those standing at the trench's edge, and then lowered to the temporary undertakers waiting in the pit. The person currently being carried along his final earthly journey is named Santo DeLeo—at least that is the name written in black marker along the side of the box. The box is not carried as evenly as the others have been; the Santo end dips precariously at the edge of the pit and it looks for a moment as if he will take a rough headfirst dive into the grave.

"Careful," says the prisoner in the pit, the older one who put his hand on the first-timer's shoulder earlier. "Respect."

"This was one fat fucker," the young prisoner trying

to pass the box into the trench says. His partner laughs and says, "Let's put him down for a second and get a better grip."

The box is lowered to the ground, a brief earthly purgatory. "You gonna help or not?" the prisoner who has been struggling says to the men behind the truck. "Here, you stand in the middle and help us balance." They all crouch over Santo DeLeo. "Now, let's lift on the count of three."

The men in the trench stand at the ready with outstretched hands. "Easy," the older one says. "Lift with your legs, pass him down easy."

The box is passed; Santo is stacked on top of a box that has no name, only the number 7,982.

"I don't think he wanted to go in there," the youngest prisoner says, and he covers his mouth again.

"Man, don't nobody want to go in there, but every man has to go in there sooner or later."

They continue their work. There are no flowers, no priest, no tombstones, no funeral attendants, just the men in steady motion passing former people into the ground.

"I'm looking for a woman who might have been buried here a few weeks ago, Arlene Lebow," Lena says to the captain. "The city morgue has lost her, but I'm told the cemetery has separate records. Could you help me find her?"

"I'll look it up in the ledger, but I can tell you, if we

buried her in the last few months, she'd be in the trench over by that oak tree. See that white marker?" He points. "That's got to be it because we just started this trench here."

"How many bod—boxes fit in one trench?"

"A hundred and fifty."

"A hundred and fifty? In one grave?"

He nods. "New Yorkers thought they were on top of each other aboveground, but if they come here, it's a hundred and fifty to a hole. Tighter than a full flophouse."

It is not a long walk to the trench, but when she stops to stand in front of the simple white cement post, she feels that she has journeyed much farther than a few miles from the city. She feels nauseated and light headed, as if she has been on a long sea voyage and is walking on unsteady feet, feeling the land underneath but with the residual sensation of being borne along the sea.

She kneels down and touches the white post, which a beetle is steadily scaling with unknown motivation. It's like a cemetery for the blind, she thinks, with no names, no dates of birth and death, all the words belowground. Above, it doesn't even look like a cemetery; the white posts could be markers for anything. And what if visitors to the dead were blindfolded and led to a tomb and told, Here, here it is—what difference would it make?

"Arlene, are you here?"

She asks herself why she came, why she feels so much sorrow for a stranger, and whether it is a form of self-pity. She looks at the unbroken landscape, the grass and trees, the clumps of blue aster, the silent, watery sound beyond. She has the sensation of being lowered, and she stands quickly, stomping her feet as if they have gone to sleep, though there hasn't been time for that. As she lifts her head, she sees a flash of tan fur in the grass, and beyond, the dark water of the sound.

"What was that, Arlene?"

What was that? she had asked one day as she rode in the car with her parents. Her mother had been very sick already, but she had wanted the three of them to go for a drive. They were still searching for him then.

"What was that?" she had asked as they drove beside the pinewoods that ran along the road.

"Where?" her mother had asked. "Where?" Her father had pulled the car to the shoulder and stopped.

"Was it the mountain lion? What did you see, Lena?"

She and her father had left her mother in the car, jumped the ditch, and entered the woods. Her father did not ask what she had seen, and when they were far enough in the woods that she couldn't see the car, she paused. In a flash she saw the mountain lion lunge as her mother opened the door and stepped out. Lena turned back toward the car and broke into a run, calling without emitting any sound.

The car door was closed, her mother safe inside. "What was it, Lena?"

"A deer, maybe."

"Do you think it was the mountain lion?"

"No, it wasn't him."

When her father came back to the car, he did not say anything, just looked at her in the rearview mirror. When she walked into the kitchen later, her mother was heating oil in the skillet while a dismembered chicken that had been dredged in flour lay on the counter like a mutilated ghost. Her father was standing at the head of the kitchen table, his hands on a rolled-up towel as he looked down at the Bible. The following Sunday his sermon was about Daniel in the lions' den. "My God hath sent his angel, and hath shut the lions' mouths, that they have not hurt me: forasmuch as before him innocency was found in me."

Remembering, Lena bows her head. "Ghost cat. Catamount. Puma. Painter. Panther. Cougar. Mountain lion," she says. "I knew all their names, Arlene. It wouldn't be the same kind of lion that devoured you. But related maybe. Crouching at my bedroom window at night, watching the dirt road that shone like a scar in the moonlight, sometimes I thought I saw him. And I thought of what it must feel like to be torn apart, to be devoured."

When she rejoins the prisoners, the captain says, "I found her burial record." He opens a ledger and shows her the page. "A. Lebow, see?"

"What are the numbers?" she asks, pointing beside the name.

"Every body gets their numbers — permit number, section number, plot number, grave number, the date the permit was issued, date of death, and the date we buried them. Careful records. Sometimes people are disinterred, and we keep records of that, too."

"Disinterred?"

"We exhume them sometimes, if their family members decide to claim them. That's why we keep records, so we can find them."

"How, exactly, do you find them?"

"See," he says, "this whole thing is laid out on a grid, like an underground city. Every trench has a number and every body has a number. So if we need to exhume one, we just match up the numbers and get them out and give them back. But they can only be exhumed within seven years of burial."

"Why seven years?"

"You have to have some cutoff, I guess. I mean, what could be left after seven years?"

She doesn't know how long it takes a body to break down, but it can't take seven years. "So, it's arbitrary?"

"I don't know about that. It's just seven years. There's got to be a statute of limitations on things, you know. At a certain point, you just have to get on with it."

They watch the men, who have finished burying and

begun digging. The trench is not full yet and they are putting the same pile of dirt and the retaining wall back in place. The youngest prisoner, with a straight black hairline that hugs his baby face, takes a string of rosary beads from his jumpsuit pocket and kisses them, then throws them in the grave.

"When we're inside," the young prisoner says, "I'm always wanting time to pass quicker, the minutes, the hours, the days, I can't stand it, ticking them off. But out here, it gives you a different—what's the word?"

"Perspective," the older prisoner says.

The rosary thrower nods. "There's different times, different pieces of it. You forget that when you're free and out on the street."

The beefy prisoner, one who was unloading coffins in the pit, takes an orange from his pocket and puts it on the ground beside the marker. The older prisoner kneels on the ground above the orange and pats his pockets.

"I don't have anything to give," he says, and the three men walk toward the morgue truck together, followed at a close distance by the corrections officer, who looks quite alone. Lena takes the brown scarf from her bag and folds it in squares, then places it under the orange.

THEY RIDE THE ferry back to City Island; the plot of beautiful land inhabited only by the dead, land within view of the city, has made them quiet and uninterested in voices and speech. Lena can't go back to Parkside. Instead, she takes the subway to Ellen Lebow's.

At the apartment building, she presses the button and waits.

"Yes?" the voice comes through the intercom.

"Ellen, it's Lena, from the *Record*. May I speak with you?"

She is buzzed in, and at the apartment door, she speaks before Ellen has invited her inside, as they are standing in the open doorway.

"Ellen, I'm here to ask your forgiveness. I lied. I do work for the *Record,* but I'm not a reporter."

"Why would you do that?"

"If you want me to leave, I will. I'm very sorry—"

Ellen pulls the door to her side and begins to slowly close it.

"But I know where she is, where Arlene's body is."

"Oh," Ellen says, stopping the door with her foot.

"She's here." She holds out the photocopy of the burial record. "She's at Hart Island. You can visit her there, and you can move her if that's what you want."

Ellen takes the paper, and Lena notices her hands: they are aged, with nicks and veins; they are the hands of a laborer. Gardener, Lena thinks. She must garden. Maybe she has a plot somewhere, a home upstate.

"Where did you get this?"

"Hart Island keeps burial records. I asked for a copy."

"You came into my home and lied to me. What were you trying to achieve? Were you just curious?"

"I met Arlene on a bus just before she died. We spoke briefly, and I remembered her when I saw her picture in the paper. Since then, I can't forget her. She haunts me. On the bus that day, we talked about the story she was reading, 'The Veldt.'"

"We read that as teenagers."

"On the bus, I had a migraine and she was trying to comfort me. It was something she did with her hands."

"Pressing? Something about pressure points?"

"Yes," Lena says. She holds out her right hand and grabs the web of skin between her thumb and index finger.

"You may as well come inside."

They pass through the foyer into the main room, and Ellen gestures for her to sit on a lumpy beige couch.

"I have no right, Ellen, I know. I just—I wish I had known her. When I read the story in the paper—"

"Whatever do you think you learn about people from a newspaper?"

"I suppose you learn things about humanity, but very little about individuals."

Ellen sits down beside her and thumps the couch cushion that sags against the armrest.

"I would have thought it's just the opposite. So, why did you lie?"

"I was trying to protect myself."

"From what?"

Lena shrugs.

"Was there anything unusual that day you met her, something that made you notice her?"

"No, she was, I don't know, ardent, attentive. We spoke briefly about 'The Veldt' and then she held my hand. It was unexpected but quite calming, a generous act. I thought at the time that I was letting her hold my hand, but afterward I realized she knew I was jittery even though I hadn't known it myself, and she was trying to soothe me."

"Was there anything else?"

She wasn't wearing a mask, Lena thinks. She looks down at the coffee table and touches the polished wood. It reminds her of the dining table at her parents' house; as a child she saw a long, leonine face in the wood's grain, an enigmatic face with dark folds near the mouth and a thick mane of hair.

"I can't explain it."

"Since she died," Ellen says, "I have the strongest sensation. It's like long periods of numbness and then a pinprick."

"That must be frightening."

"I'd be more frightened if I never felt the prick."

"You mean because you'd remain numb?"

"Or maybe I'd forget how to fear." Outside the bay

window, a boat on the Hudson looks like a toy, moving and yet seeming almost static.

"What do you think the prick is?"

"I don't know. God maybe. Except I'm an academic, an agnostic, and yet . . ." She shrugs. "God. The word is so strange to me. Do you have any faith?"

"No, not anymore." She stands awkwardly, looking down at Ellen's bent head, her part showing the white of her scalp like a chalk line.

"Ellen, that day I saw Arlene on the bus, I thought perhaps I recognized something."

"Recognized what?"

"I don't know how to explain it. That something had gone wrong. That she knew. That she knew where we were both going. That it was there somehow, on her face, written, as she read with her fingertips. I thought I saw my life there, my past and my future. I know it sounds stupid."

Ellen looks up at her. "It's not a matter of stupidity."

"It was as if she knew and was trying to tell me that words can't insulate. Language can't save you. You have to live with your head in the lion's mouth."

"But she didn't choose life."

"She did, for a moment."

"You don't think you could have saved her."

"No, it's not that. When I said I recognized something, it was an expression, a look, that I have only seen once before."

"What kind of expression?"

"An expression on my mother's face shortly before she died. I had asked her something and her answer was that look. But I don't know if it was grace, or resignation."

"Which do you think it was?"

"I don't know. I suppose I'll never know."

CHAPTER THIRTEEN

WMDs Still Missing

Lena stops by the *Record* to see whether her absence has been noticed, but it hasn't. Out of the office all day and no one knows. There are no calls on the overnight machine; no tapes have been dropped in the mail slot. She leaves the office and begins to shake as she walks west, the opposite of her usual route, and as she looks at the people she passes, it seems that the street is a concrete canal that has been drained and has exposed them there, walking along the bottom. This is so disconcerting that she enters the bar on the corner, the *Record* hangout.

Once again, Katheryn is there, clutching Russell as she holds court. Once again, he smiles at something she says and lifts his head to glance around the room. When his eyes meet Lena's, she nods and looks away.

She orders a scotch and tries to act the way people must mean when they say "normal."

"How are you?" Russell asks, approaching the bar. His voice sounds different, though she couldn't say how. She closes her eyes briefly. "Lena," he says, and she doesn't know whether she could identify his voice on tape, a shocking realization.

"How was DC?"

"DC is fabulous," Katheryn says loudly, coming to stand beside Russell. "Did Russell tell you? He's the new deputy bureau chief in Washington. One step away from bureau chief, and we all know what comes after Washington."

"I wanted to tell you, Lena, it just happened and there was no time."

"Congratulations."

He looks down at the floor and then up at her with that Russell expression, boyish and endearing.

"When do you move?"

"Next week. I'm going down this weekend to look for a place."

Katheryn rubs his back and Russell grimaces. It's all there, so much more seen in a glance than in a gaze: it is the look of panic that leads to paralysis. He has submitted to her.

"I've been trying to convince him to stay at my place until he finds something," Katheryn says, moving her hand to his arm. "You know I've got that big place in Georgetown, and I'm going to be spending more time there myself. It'd be nice to have some company. And Washington's viperous; I could show Russell the ropes."

Lena watches him try to think of what to say. She wants to kiss him, he wants to speak; they both open their mouths.

"I have to go," she says, and in one ungraceful movement she tosses money on the bar and slides off the barstool.

She is tempted to push past people on her way to the door, to shove them, but she doesn't because at the same time she doesn't want to be touched. The street is surprisingly empty; the humid air smells of sweat, as if city sidewalks, which have been absorbing sweat all summer, finally reached saturation and threw the water back up in the air.

MORNING IN THE Recording Room: all is orderly and silent.

Though there are no tapes to transcribe, she puts on her headphones and presses the foot pedal.

Silence slips in her ear like a mute tongue. The door opens.

"Yo? Excuse me."

It is Lance, a magazine writer. He has slightly long, shaggy brown hair and wears black chunky glasses and, on Fridays, his *Nation* T-shirt. When he's feeling particularly subversive, he wears a long-sleeved T-shirt under the short-sleeved one. On all days, he addresses everyone under the age of sixty—which, at the *Record,* is fewer people than one might imagine—as "Yo."

He hands Lena his taped interview with a diminutive pop star whose "life goals" are to design furniture and fit into the framed James Brown jacket that hangs above his ostrich-feather lamp. As she transcribes, the pop star explains that his furniture designs are based on circles "because, you know, circles are so sensual."

"Are you a Virgo?" Lance asks.

Lena stops typing, takes off the headphones.

"I can't do this anymore," she says out loud. "Arlene, I can't do it either."

A knock at the door makes her jump. "Just push it open, the door handle's broken." She turns. "Oh. Russell."

"Lena."

He pulls a chair from under one of the unused desks and sits down.

"Ellen Lebow called. She said you visited her twice, and that the first time you said you were a reporter."

"I did."

Russell leans back, rubs his smooth face. "What the hell were you thinking, Lena?"

"It seems dishonest, but I didn't feel dishonest, only that I was using the tools at hand."

"You know you could be fired, Lena. You know this is serious."

"Yes, it is serious."

She knows that he feels compromised, here to assess the damage to the *Record,* and also annoyed that he is personally implicated, tainted by association. Russell values clarity and detests equivocation.

"I don't know who you are, Lena. This is a betrayal of the *Record,* of me, of the profession of reporting. We're out there every day, trying to be honest, trying to be objective, gathering information—"

"There is no objectivity, Russell. You observe information. I register it. I'm the one hooked to a machine, I'm the cord. You and Katheryn might be the organs, but I'm the vein."

They are able to look at each other with frankness now, recognizing that they do not balance each other, that their passions run counter to each other's, as do their principles.

"Nothing changes the fact that you lied."

"It was a sin of omission."

"The worst kind."

"Like Eric Isaacs?"

"What?"

"I know he's been kidnapped. When you lied to me, was that a sin of omission?"

"You understand why I didn't tell you, right?"

"Because you want to control the information. Because you trust yourself with it, but not others."

"That's not fair."

"That's how you and Katheryn are similar."

"Lena, all reporters are like that. There's no comparison here between what you did and what I did. You've put me in a bad position. I'm not going to report it, but we can't see each other anymore. I can't be involved."

There is nothing unfinished between them, but something from their encounter is stored inside them both, has graced them. She smiles at the thought that the *Record* would scorn such a word, *grace*.

After Russell leaves, she stands at the phone panel and fiddles absentmindedly with the recorders.

"I don't know what to do." She presses "record" on one of the Dictaphones. "I. don't. know." Stop. Rewind. Record. "Don't know." She takes the mudslide tape from the cardboard box. Fast forward. Play. ". . . digging the next day, and the next, and the day after that, and for as long as it would take . . . not leave anyone behind."

They did not grow wise, invented no song,
devised for themselves no sort of language.
They dug.

At her desk, she ejects Lance's tape from her Dicta-phone and tugs on the tape at the bottom of the cassette. So fragile, so easy to make the plastic spill its guts. She yanks harder and more tape unspools in her hand. "Ha." She winds it around her palm, circling the flesh until it looks like a fighter's wrap. Then she continues to pull until she holds the entire tape in her hand.

The recording phone rings, and after a slight hesitation she answers; Katheryn is at JFK and wants to dictate a story before her flight.

"Am I sending the transcript to the foreign desk?"

"No, listen to me Lena, don't send it to the foreign desk. Send it to Ralph. He'll know what to do. Dateline: With the Seventh Marine Regiment, near Baghdad, July nineteenth."

Lena presses the button on the receiver that allows her to speak on the recording line. "That's the dateline?"

"Yes. Is there a problem?"

"I thought you were in New York."

"Look, I was in Baghdad, right? And I just got this information, so obviously I'm not going back to Bagh-dad to do a fucking toe touch for the dateline. I'm at the airport, at the gate, and Ralph is in the page one meeting. I want you to do your job. Just type this up and send it to Ralph. Is that clear?"

"Yes."

"Good. Starting dictation now. Lead: An adviser who defected from Saddam Hussein's regime said that he had evidence of bunkers inside Iraq that served as bioweapons labs stop. The defector comma whose identity has not been revealed for safety reasons comma showed members of the Seventh Marines a blueprint of a bunker that he said contained the materials for building chemical weapons stop. End Graph."

Lena rewinds the lead, puts on her headset, and watches her hands hover over the keyboard. Her fingers refuse to touch the letters. She presses the foot pedal and stares down at the escape hood that is still perched on top of the trash can.

"Reusable?" she says aloud, bending down to read the box and once again reading the instructions. "In the event of emergency, simply attach the filter, pull the hood down over your head, and tighten the straps."

She lifts the hood out of the box, pulls it over her head, sits again, and presses the foot pedal. Through the hood's eyeholes, she watches her fingers pass over the keys.

"When asked why he chose to defect comma the adviser said comma quote The point of life is not to just go on living stop end quote."

Lifting her foot from the pedal, she throws off the hood. She has rewound the tape and is listening to the quote again when the phone rings.

"Hi, Lena. It's Katheryn. Look, don't send that story to Ralph. We have to kill it."

"Why?"

"Don't worry about why. It's complicated. Suffice it to say that there's some delicate material in there that the Pentagon isn't ready to publish."

"You showed it to the Pentagon?"

"Lena, you don't understand how this works. I want you to erase the tape. And then I want you to delete anything you've typed. Do you understand? This has to do with the sensitive nature of the information. We have to hold it for a few days, that's all. Shit, they're calling my flight, I have to go. I just wanted to make sure you destroy the tape."

"I'm afraid I can't destroy the tape, Katheryn. I have to keep a record of all the calls. It's already logged."

"Listen to me. Do you have any idea of my position? Do you have any idea what it's like to be embedded with the military? Do you have any idea what it's like to search for something as dangerous as WMDs?"

"Yes, I think I do."

"How could you? You don't know. It's not like you were there!"

"I know about searching."

"That's ridiculous. Fuck. They're calling my flight. Kill the story and I'll come by and get the tape when I'm back in town on Tuesday."

Lena puts the phone back in its cradle. She finishes transcribing the tape and sends the transcript to the foreign desk. In exactly fifteen minutes she calls the foreign editor. "Hi, this is Lena in the Recording Room. I sent something from Katheryn Keel a few minutes ago."

"We got it, thanks."

"I just wanted to make sure it was slotted. Katheryn said she's getting on a plane and won't land before deadline."

"Well, isn't that convenient? I was just in the page one meeting and Ralph was holding space for it on A one."

"I just wanted to check. She was adamant that it not be held because she was unreachable."

"I'm sure it will run."

"Thanks."

Lena raises the window and leans out on the ledge, beside the pigeon. "We're supposed to eat the evidence," she says, slapping the tape against her palm.

She leans farther over the ledge. "It's nice up here, isn't it? Up above it all," she says softly.

The pigeon turns its puny head from the street to the sky, as if to say, All this. They look down at Times Square, where pedestrians wander under the nonstop neon.

"What am I going to do?"

Times Square is thick with tourists and the noise of traffic and people haggling over handbags and the cost of chalk portraits. She is halfway down the block when the fifty-cent lady steps out, extends her hand like a weary landlady, and says, "Fifty cents."

"Hi, Lydia."

She stops and Lydia looks at her, eyes cloudy with cataracts and suspicion. Lena takes a dollar from her wallet and holds it out, but Lydia regards it in silence and does not reach for it.

Again, she thinks of Electra: "Each night that dies with dawn / I bring my sad songs here."

A veined hand with long, tapered fingers reaches out finally for the dollar. Her fingers are thin and elegant, ravaged by age and yet containing still the traces of supple youth.

"Your hands—" Lena says with surprise, "you have such nice hands."

Lydia looks down at her hands and smiles. "He always loved my hands," she says. "I could reach over an octave."

"Did you play the piano?"

The mask snaps back into place. "Go away," Lydia says sharply.

Lena is still thinking of the woman who lost her name when, at the intersection of Forty-Third and Broadway, a careering cab and a messenger bike collide with the terrible but perfect choreography of crashing that sends the cyclist through the air, over the taxi's hood, and thudding on his back to the filthy street.

Even though Lena makes her living by listening, she could never describe the sound of impact that causes one to instinctively turn one's head. It is the sound of two things coming together that should not, the sound that everyone recognizes, the sound of solid meeting solid and stopping.

Times Square slows and swirls and, for Lena, goes silent. Of course, it doesn't, it couldn't, it wouldn't. The men who hawk handbags probably don't turn their boom boxes down. The traffic, of tourists and taxis, can't have stopped. People just across the street probably don't see, don't hear, and keep going, not knowing what is there for them to witness, just as the ship sailed smoothly on when Icarus fell from the sky.

The cyclist lies on his back, his legs extended straight, as if he were stretching after yoga. The driver steps out of the cab, stunned, and stands behind the half-open door with one foot still in the car. He doesn't advance but leans on the door as if for protection. "Not my fault," he says. "Not my fault," he repeats, clutching the door.

Cars honk behind him, then pull around. Lena steps off the curb and drops to her knees beside the cyclist. He is not bleeding, but his stillness in the middle of Times Square is more disquieting than blood. Maybe his neck is broken, or his spine. She says the empty phrase that one says to reassure the dying, but mostly to reassure the witness. "It's going to be all right."

The cyclist does not move his head but blinks his eyes and says seven heartbreaking words. "Will you take my helmet off, please?"

The question takes her by surprise, the sweet simplicity of it, the need to be unencumbered before death. He is young and beautiful, his muscles tense, his skin tan.

"I shouldn't move you," she says. "You shouldn't move."

A heavy young guy in calf-length shorts and a Lakers jersey is talking on his cell phone as he walks down Broadway, and his eyes lock with Lena's as she glances up in search of help.

"Yo, dog!" he says into the phone. "Mad shit." And then, with a gesture that he has probably never used before but maybe saw in a movie once, he delicately covers the mouthpiece of his cell phone, pinkie slightly raised, and says to Lena, "Is he dead?"

She looks down at the cyclist, who says something she cannot hear. She leans down, turning her head so that her ear is so close to his mouth she can feel his warm breath, which smells faintly of the sea. He is quietly pleading now. "Please take my helmet off."

"Oh," she says, looking at him and trying to smile. "I better not do that. I shouldn't move your neck."

His golden-brown hair curls around the edges of his helmet; he reminds her of Rilke's Apollo with his legendary head, his eyes gleaming like ripening fruit.

She looks up at the surreal scene, where most people do not seem to notice that a man is dying in the street.

"Call nine one one!" she shouts to the guy on the sidewalk, who is still talking on his phone.

"Aww," he says, "I'm talking to my man in the pen. Can't you call?"

"No, I can't call."

"Well, why fucking not?"

"Because I don't have a fucking cell phone."

"What, you lose it?"

"No, I don't have one."

"Mad shit!" He lifts his arms in the air, then doubles over in disbelief. "This girl ain't fucking got no fucking cell phone."

"Hey," she shouts, "someone's dying before your eyes! Fucking call nine fucking one one!"

The guy bends at the waist, and when his sneakered foot slips off the curb, he quickly yanks it back. "Well, fuck," he says, "all you had to do was fucking say so." He grips the phone and glares at Lena. "Yo, man, I got to go. This lady here ain't got no fucking phone, so I got to call nine one one." She watches as he pulls the phone away from his ear and dramatically presses the button to end the call. He presses three buttons and turns away. "Forty-Third and Broadway," he is saying into the phone.

The cyclist suddenly sits up and removes his helmet. Lena touches his arm. "Are you sure you should do that? An ambulance will be here soon."

He rubs his sweaty curls. "I'm OK," he says. He starts to stand.

"But how . . . wait, you were . . . why don't you sit down on the curb?"

He brushes himself off and leans over, hands on knees. "My bike," he says, picking it up and feeling it like a doctor feeling for fractures. "My bike," he says again. "I think my bike is fine. Unbelievable." He straightens and smiles. "I really think I'm OK."

"Hold on—why don't you wait for the ambulance? I'll wait with you. You could have a concussion or something. And the cab driver . . ." She turns, but the driver is already in his cab and, in a show of newfound timidity, has his turn signal on and is attempting to merge back into traffic. He waves to them and squeezes the taxi into the moving lane of cars.

The cyclist throws his leg over the bike. "Thanks," he says, and then he is gone.

Lena thinks she may have to sit down on the curb to recover from this Times Square miracle, but the ambulance arrives and she has to explain to two tired medics why she is the only person left at the scene of an accident.

She tries to say something as the medics turn away, but no words will come. She opens her mouth and says in a voice she doesn't recognize, "He almost died. Right here, in the middle of Times Square, in the middle of all these people, right in front of us.

"Do something!" she yells. No one has heard; the ambulance doors close, the siren goes silent, and the van pulls away.

She stands on the sidewalk and looks at the street where the cyclist had been. Life had changed in an instant and then changed back again. Cars drive on, and some of the tires must be circling over the exact spot where just moments earlier a man lay dying and then not dying. She looks at the people pushing past, at the tickertape flowing above their heads, and above that, at the giant models looking down on them from the safety of their flat-screen boxes, mirrors to the impossible, taunting the tourists with the world of manufactured beauty.

Staring at the empty accident scene, Lena again sees the cyclist, his beautiful body lying still in the street, his lithe legs, his torso like Apollo's, lit from within.

CHAPTER FOURTEEN

Are We Kings or
Are We Dogs?

In the morning, she buys a paper at the neighborhood coffee shop, where the Italian men continue to sit under the green awning discussing the merits of being born wealthy or handsome.

Katheryn's article is on A1: IRAQI DEFECTOR CLAIMS KNOWLEDGE OF BIOWEAPONS BUNKERS. It is almost exactly as Katheryn dictated on the tape that Lena has in her pocket. She is sure she will be fired, but she has to face it, so she walks to work as usual.

The security guards either have not been alerted or do not associate her physical modesty with the rogue worker they have been told to watch for, so they smile as she swipes her card and enters the elevator bank.

In the Recording Room, she presses the flashing light on the overnight machine, and Katheryn's unmistakable voice screams, "I will have you fired! This is your last day at the *Record*. You will never be affiliated with this institution again!"

Lena laughs at the last line. "It's a country of bureaucrats," she says as she erases Katheryn's voice from the machine.

"Yo," Lance says from the open doorway.

"Yo."

"I wondered if you had that transcript yet."

"I called the desk last night but they said you had already left. The tape was completely blank, Lance, completely clean. There was nothing on it."

"For real?"

"For real. I'm sorry. Did you have it near something magnetic?"

"Oh, shit, I don't think so."

"I hope you have good notes."

"Oh, fuck. Who takes notes anymore? Can I at least get the tape back?"

"I put it in interoffice mail. Since it was blank, I figured—"

"I better go down to the mailroom. We still have a mailroom, right?"

"On the sixth floor."

"Thanks."

After Lance leaves, she turns off her computer and, using the office phone, dials the recording line. There are three rings; then the overnight machine picks up with a click, and the sound of her own voice fills the room: "You have reached the Recording Room's dictation mailbox. Please note that this voice mailbox has a maximum duration of twenty minutes . . ."

She erases this message and records a new one: "You have reached the *Record*'s Recording Room. This is the transcriptionist speaking. Please do not dictate your story. It will not be transcribed. The transcriptionist will transcribe no more. Do you hear me? I hope so, because I've heard you. I've listened for four years, through news—breaking, boring, and mundane. And this is what I've learned: that silence has two sounds, one high, one low, the sound of the central nervous system and the hum of blood circulating. Listen for it now. Listen for the lower frequencies."

Looking around the room as though for the first time, she views it with some distance, some degree of objective scrutiny. The room is small, shabby, familiar; she will not feel any sadness at leaving it. There is only one question, one asked by many when returning to the town where they are born: Why did it take me so long to leave?

There is a soft knock on the door.

"Come in."

It's one of the security guards she has been nodding

hello and good-bye to for four years. She remembers when his wife died two years ago because one night in the lobby he showed her a forty-year-old picture of the two of them at Brighton Beach.

"Tommy."

He is tall and ruddy, Irish, a retired cop. They both blush.

"Lena?"

"Yes."

"I have to"—he looks down and clasps his hands in em-barrassment—"I have to escort you to Howard's office."

"Sure. I understand."

"And he said to bring the tape."

"What tape?"

"He said you would know. He says it's urgent."

They take the elevator to the silent fourteenth floor. It is the only carpeted floor in the building; the beige mate-rial muffles footsteps completely, and she is reminded of how prison guards used to cover their shoes with socks to silence footsteps in the solitary confinement ward.

When Lena enters, the young woman at the reception desk in the outer office glances up and gives her a look of stern reproach, which she perfected during her year abroad at Oxford. Lena busies herself looking around the room. It is boring except for a bookshelf full of books by *Record* writers. On the modern glass coffee table is a carefully arranged yo-yo collection.

"You can go in now."

Tommy hesitates at the receptionist's silent stare. "I'll go now. Good luck to you, Lena."

"Thanks, Tommy."

She approaches Howard's office door, which is half-closed, and looks in. He sits in his ergonomically advanced chair with his back to the door and does not immediately turn even though she clears her throat when she enters.

"Trust in the *Record* is everything. It is the paper of record," he says, spinning around. He is a bit short for such a high-backed chair, but he is not wearing critter suspenders; he has a pleasant, youthful, almost kind face. "People do trust it. And they should. And I—we—want them to. And you, Lena, have damaged that trust."

His face is slightly pink, unthreatening. He motions for her to sit down. The bookshelf beside his desk displays books on management, the Middle East, and golf and, on the middle shelf, more yo-yos.

"I damaged the *Record*'s trust with readers, or the *Record*'s trust with the Pentagon?"

"Lena, I'm trying to do you a favor here. Katheryn Keel has been on the phone all morning, practically clawing through the line to get at you. Have you ever seen this woman angry?" he asks, patting his face. "I'm surprised my eyebrows weren't singed off."

Lena shields her eyes against the strong sunlight coming through the window behind him. Sky is all that can be seen at this height, stretches of sky and pieces of other, taller buildings.

"Now I need you to hand over the tape with Katheryn's dictation. I don't want to make this any more painful than it already is. A security guard will escort you to Human Resources, where they'll go over your severance package."

"I take responsibility for what I did. But you've got a foreign reporter who passes her copy to the Pentagon for approval, not to mention the issue of fraudulent datelines."

"Lena, Katheryn Keel is a legendary reporter. Now I need that tape."

"I'm sorry. I don't think that's the most ethical action here."

"Ethical action? I'm not sure you understand my position. This could be incredibly damaging for us. And as far as organizations go, we're at the top of the heap, so to speak. And there are always those interested in knocking the king off the mountain."

"Yes, the *Record* is definitely at the top of the heap."

He tilts his head, suspicious. "What do you mean?"

"Just that it's true. As my father used to say, no one kicks a dead dog."

"Yes, Lena, this dog is very much at the top of the heap."

"Some would argue that all newspapers are pretty dead dogs. But I assure you that I don't kick dogs, living or dead."

"One could say you have disgraced the king of the mountain. You—"

As he continues his surreal talk about disgraced kings and dead dogs, Lena examines his smooth, fair-skinned face. We sit here across from each other, she wants to say, and yet you have not read your own obit. But it has been written. Howard is expected to live many more years, but the advance obit is on file, as it is for many newsworthy people, just in case. It is well known that he is an adventure-seeking vacationer, and it would take only one false move with the telemark boots or a faulty parachute cord to land him on page 1 with that unmistakable headline including his age, which will never change once it has been set in 24-point Record New Roman font.

"—what kind do you think the *Record* would be, Lena?"

"I'm afraid I don't get your meaning. What are you asking?"

"I said what kind do you think the *Record* would be, you know, standing at the top of the heap at the top of the mountain?"

She tries to grasp the conversational thread. He could mean which king does the *Record* represent, the king of the mountain. Or he could mean what kind of dog would be at the top of the heap.

"I'm sorry, Howard. Are you talking about—are we kings or are we dogs?"

"That, Lena," he says, thumping his desk, "is the question of our time. Are we kings or are we dogs?"

"It is a question I often ponder myself."

"I think, Lena, that as far as dogs go, the *Record* would be a cross between a Saint Bernard and—what was that Lassie dog?"

"A collie."

"That's it! The *Record,* the dog at the top of the heap, would be a kind of Lassie–Saint Bernard, saving the wayward and bounding home in victory."

A sound from behind causes her to turn toward a figure in the doorway. She doesn't recognize him at first; he stands very still and straight, with a regal, almost military bearing.

"Dad!" Howard shouts. "What are you doing here?"

"Hello, Son."

"Kov?" Lena asks. "You're Popcorn?"

"I never told you my full name, Lena. Kolvin Hirn."

"Kolvin Hirn, the publisher of the *Record*?"

"Former publisher. My son is the publisher now."

"Dad, what are you doing here?"

"Howard, you know I have not interfered since I retired."

Howard has moved to the edge of his desk and is nervously catching and releasing one of the yo-yos.

"That's true, Dad. And I appreciate it. But this just isn't a good time. Let's talk later."

"It can't wait. I'm here about Lena."

She looks from Kov to Howard in shock. They look nothing alike, the son small but round faced in an overlarge suit, the father lean and angular in a button-down shirt, unwrinkled but worn, a distinct formality about him.

"Kov, why didn't you tell me?"

"I'm sorry, Lena. It wasn't intentional, not at first anyway. The day you found me in my hiding place, I didn't want to blow my cover. Yes, it was dishonest, and I'm sorry for that, but I didn't want to scare you away, to silence you."

"How do you two know each other?" Howard asks, clenching the yo-yo in his fist. "And what do you mean, your 'hiding place'?"

"I've been archiving the obituaries, the paper copies."

"Dad, we talked about this. It's unnecessary. You should be enjoying retirement. We decided."

"You decided. I decided something different. I enjoy working with the obits—"

"But Dad, it's not worthy of you. It's not important."

"Obits mark the lives that define us as a nation; they embody the moral imperative of the newspaper, one that is slipping away."

"It's a memento, Dad. It's—"

"It is not a memento. It is memorialization. And Lena understands this; she literally serves as a connector within the paper. I will not allow you to fire her. I will not allow it."

"You will not undermine me," Howard says, his voice quivering. "I'm the publisher now. It is not your decision. She defied Katheryn Keel. We've got a story on A one that the Pentagon is denying and the White House . . . you don't even want to know about the White House. I can have the board—"

"If you fire Lena, you have to fire Katheryn."

"You can't be serious."

"By your own logic, they both violated the *Record*'s rules. I've expressed before my reservations about Katheryn's reporting, her sources. But she agreed to have her work vetted by the Pentagon. That's not—"

"Dad, Katheryn was cleared."

"What do you mean, cleared? You knew the Pentagon was censoring—"

"It's not censorship, Dad. It's a different kind of war we're in now. We have to adapt to the times."

"We're not fighting a war, Howard. We are running a newspaper."

"We're on the front lines."

"That is nonsense. You sound like Ralph. Is that where this is coming from?"

"We got eight Pulitzers last year under Ralph!"

"You don't buy Pulitzers with censorship!"

"Excuse me," Lena says. "I'm sure you two have things to discuss in private. Kov, I really appreciate what you're trying to do, but it's not necessary. I want to leave the *Record*. I'm ready. I want to leave."

They both stare at her, and for the first time she sees the father-son similarity in their expression of surprise. Howard must once have been under his father's wing, acquiring the self-assurance and certainty that has allowed him to chart his own course.

Without another word, she crosses the room and holds out her hand to Howard, who, susceptible to political and even civilian instinct, shakes it.

She turns to leave. "Where are you going? I need that tape!" Howard shouts, but Kov steps in front of him, and Lena makes her escape. As she hurries down the hall, she does not feel nervous; she feels a lightness, a lightness so unfamiliar that she supposes it must be freedom, or almost freedom, or at least more freedom than she has felt in years.

She reaches the Recording Room unnoticed. It takes less than five minutes to pack her belongings — *Merriam-Webster's* tenth edition, the *Record* style manual, the escape hood that still sits on top of the trash can — and less time to unpack them. She won't take anything.

From her desk drawer, she removes a pair of green

rubber gloves and pulls them on. When she holds her arms out to open the window, she stops and stares at her covered hands, which look oddly detached, dismembered, masked.

The pigeon is not alarmed when she raises the window and steps out beside him. The ledge is extended but it is not a full balcony. *Balconette*—the word finally comes to her. That's what it's called. Like a resistance fighter about to be caught, she unfolds the clipping about Arlene and tears it to pieces, the paper soft as breadcrumbs from heat and handling. She places the pieces on the ledge, where a hot breeze lifts the remains and releases them to the city below.

The pigeon is not fazed. He has probably seen more shocking things. There is no need to speak aloud, but Lena feels that she can speak silently to the pigeon and, through him, to Arlene, to her mother, to the city below, and in that way everything that needs to be understood will be.

"What does it look like through a bird's eyes?" He stands sentry, facing the shabby hotel across the street. He does not look left toward Times Square, or right toward the Hudson. The city sounds are muted, the activity suspended, everything suspended.

"Is that the way to do it?" she asks out loud. "Straight ahead, no distraction from the periphery." She looks toward the river. It is as if she is in a hot-air balloon, hovering over the city, drifting, observing. Looking down, she feels that she could never be one of the ones who has jumped, yet, at the same time, that she already has.

"I never said I would take you," she says, even as she reaches for him. The pigeon is startled and struggles quietly, the only sound his flapping wings. She realizes for the first time that she does not know whether pigeons have a song or whether they are able to sound a single note.

"Come on, come on." She tries to think of the proper way to hold a bird, but she has no idea. She must have held one before at least once in her life, but if so, she cannot remember. The bird puts up a valiant struggle, for something that weighs less than a pound. Finally, she wraps a gloved hand around his back and rests her fingers on his breast. "Shh," she says, twisting awkwardly to stroke his feathered head with her right hand.

Across the street, a man sticks his head out his hotel room window. He has burnt-blond hair and a sagging face that might have been handsome once. The window is dirty, its dingy curtains yellowing, and she sees it with the same remove with which she saw the Recording Room earlier. She feels light and detached and almost asks him, How do we stand such unwelcoming rooms? How did I?

He leans out farther and she sees he is shirtless and

paunchy, flabby but not fat. He holds out his hands in the universal sign for "slow down." "You're not going to jump, are you, lady? It can't be that bad. You need help? You want me to call somebody?"

Their voices carry surprisingly easily above the street, like voices over water.

"No," she answers. "It's the pigeon."

"He's a bird. It's all right if he jumps. They can fly."

She nods and smiles, grips the pigeon tighter. He has paused in his furious flapping, as if listening to their conversation.

"Oh, honey, I wouldn't mess with him if I was you," he calls. "Flying rats, they carry disease and shit."

"Thanks."

"I've got to say. I've seen some weird shit in my day, but I've never seen nobody trying to save a damn pigeon, much less go out on a window ledge to do it. You sure you don't need something?"

"No, but thanks. I appreciate it."

Suddenly, red-nailed fingers creep around the man's waist from behind. A woman's head emerges under his arm. Her hair has dark roots and she has a hard face made harder with the mask of makeup visible even from across the street.

"That's nasty," she says, looking at the pigeon.

"You don't want me to call nobody?" the man says. "You don't need any help?"

"No. It's fine, really."

"You be careful up there, now."

"I will. Thank you."

He gives her one last look and shakes his head, and the red-tipped fingers draw him back into the dark room.

Lena grips the pigeon tighter as they resume their silent struggle. With a jerk, she tries to lift him, and then she sees. His left foot is caught in a tiny crack in the concrete. She is so stunned by his tattered, bloody leg that she releases him and cries out.

"Oh. I didn't know."

The Recording Room window slams shut behind them and they both start. She is fully on the ledge now, shut out in every way.

"Come on, let me see." She tries to look at the pigeon's mangled leg without touching him. "How long have you been like that? You stoic little beast."

She reaches over and gently lifts him an inch. His eyes seem redder than usual and she releases him suddenly, thinking for one terrible moment that he is going to cry. Impossible, she tells herself. Pigeons can't sing, they can't cry, they may even be deaf.

"Impossible," she says aloud. "I can't save you. There's nothing I can do."

Everything below is muffled, and there seems to be a pattern to it all as she peers down from above: pedestrians, traffic, the entire scene. It is here on the ledge that she feels her body begin to empty out. All the passages she's memorized to fill the space inside, all the thousands of feet of tape she's transcribed. It is as if all the words are leaving her, the incessant tape is spooling out of her, through her open mouth, through her pores. She feels the letters streaming out through her fingertips, and she can finally be empty.

"Pigeon," she repeats, "there's really nothing more I can do for you."

There is a tap behind her, and Tommy raises the window and cries, "Don't jump, Lena! For the love of Mary, don't jump."

She holds her hands in the air. "It's OK, Tommy."

"It's not worth it," he pleads. "It's not even a fun place to work anymore."

"I'm not going to jump."

He motions for her to come inside and backs away from the open window to give her room. She looks at her hands and begins to remove the gloves, pulling at the green shadow fingers one by one to loosen them, then tugging the gloves off by the fingertips.

"If I leave you, you'll die, and if I take you, you'll die," she says to the pigeon.

Tommy doesn't hear but looks at the gloves, seeming to notice them only now, only after she has removed them and holds them, the limp and empty fingers dangling from her grip. He crouches in front of the window, holding his stiff back and squinting behind his glasses.

"It's the pigeon," she says, gesturing with the empty gloves. "He's caught. It's his leg."

"You came out on this window ledge for a pigeon?"

"It's his leg," she repeats, feeling foolish. "He's stuck."

Tommy leans his big red-haired head out the window. "Well, don't touch him," he says gently. "He might have germs."

"He's hurt, Tommy. And he's trapped. I can't get his leg loose without amputating it."

"Well, leave him there for now," Tommy says. "We'll call pest control or somebody."

"Pest control?"

"Oh boy, oh boy, oh boy," he says, backing into the room. "Lena, we don't have much time."

"I'm sorry. I didn't mean to—"

He shakes his head. "Tell you what. We need to get you out of here. Why don't we focus on that?"

"Thank you, Tommy," she says. He gently holds her elbow as she steps through the window and back into the room. "I'm ready."

"I can help you carry your things downstairs."

"I'm not taking anything."

"Oh, come on, you must want something. Here's a stylebook"—he holds up the familiar white-jacketed guide—"a stapler"—he lifts it up in the air. She shakes her head. "Scissors!" he says. "These are good ones, they're heavy. You can trim rosebushes with these."

"Just one thing," she says, grabbing the orange box from the trash. "I want my escape hood."

A voice comes over Tommy's walkie-talkie and he lifts it with his rough, freckled hand. "Come in, Tommy. This is the command chief at the command center. Have you located the transcriptionist? Over."

"This is Tommy reporting to the command center," he says, winking at Lena. "I have located the transcriptionist and will personally escort her out of the building. All is calm and under control, over."

"OK. Howard ordered us all to drop everything, but we've got the secretary of state in the executive dining room and one of the bomb-sniffing dogs just puked on the carpet, so we're kinda busy. But let us know if you need reinforcements. Over."

She shakes his hand.

"Good luck, Lena."

"Tommy, one last thing. I know I'm not in a position to be asking favors, but if you could just leave the pigeon on the ledge. I know someone in the building I can call to take care of it."

"I don't see any harm in that."

"Thank you."

She pulls the escape hood over her head and fastens it

snugly. People in the hall turn to look at her as she passes; they laugh, then go silent when she doesn't respond. In the lobby, she puts her ID on the security desk as the guards watch in astonishment. Outside, it is a humid summer day, and she breathes heavily inside the hood.

A man wearing several layers of clothes slumps beside the building. "Yesterday was a new day," he says. "But today is old already." Lena is too preoccupied to turn away, and they make eye contact. His face is pallid, sweat-sheened. She nods and tries to smile. Just then a dog walks by, unusual for this neighborhood, and lunges toward the man. The dog strains at its leash but does not bark, sniffs instead, curious about the smell. If a pack of wild dogs were released on the streets of Manhattan, Lena thinks, the homeless would be the ones spared.

A few feet farther and the hand emerges from behind the column. She takes the tape with Katheryn's dictation and presses it into Lydia's hand, which she covers with her own. Lydia nods with solemnity and leans forward in a gesture somewhere between a nod and a bow.

Lena turns onto Broadway, ignoring the shouts and laughter the escape hood elicits as she joins the masses walking under blinking billboards and tickertapes, numbed by neon, walking north, just walking.

CHAPTER FIFTEEN

Arlene Lebow Dies
at Fifty-Four

In her stuffy Parkside room, she lies down and immediately falls asleep. In the dark, when she wakens, tangled in the sweat-dampened sheets, she jumps up and reaches for the phone. She dials the familiar voice and listens to the new instructions, her own.

"Arlene, I'm calling to say good-bye. You didn't really disappear, after all. Your sister knows where to find you. And I didn't vanish either, though I was afraid I would. For the longest time I thought the tapes were spooling within me, invading, spreading. I thought soon I would not possess a single thought of my own, would not possess even my own dreams. But I was wrong. Listening doesn't make us disappear. It just helps us recognize our absurdity, our humanity. It's what binds us together, as the newspaper binds us and before that Chaucer's tales and before that the Scriptures."

IN THE MORNING, as she emerges from the dining room with a contraband coffee mug, Mrs. Pelletier calls to her.

"I'm sorry," she says, looking at the mug. "I know we're not supposed to take things out of the dining—"

"Lena," Mrs. Pelletier says, "your uncle is waiting for you in the front parlor."

"My uncle? I don't—"

Mrs. Pelletier leans over the counter. "I can see the family resemblance," she says, lifting her hands and framing the upper half of her face. "It's in the eyes."

In the parlor, Kov is sitting on the plastic-covered settee. His lips are pressed together; his straight gray hair is slicked back from his forehead.

"Hello, Uncle."

He lifts the lid from the box at his side and she sees the pigeon, who glares at her with the glazed eyes of a newborn.

"He should survive. We're just back from the clinic.

They had to amputate," he says, pointing to the tiny tourniquet around the string-size leg.

"The two of you are staying together?"

"Just until the wound heals. They're quite speedy healers—have to be, I suppose."

"Kov, why don't we take a walk in Gramercy Park? I can get the key."

He stands and straightens, gracefully offers her his arm. She links her arm through his and they walk to the front desk.

"Mrs. Pelletier, may I check out a key to the park?"

"Is your uncle going with you? How nice."

Mrs. Pelletier heaves the black Book of Keys onto the desk and Lena signs her name. She replaces the pen chained to the counter, then immediately picks it back up and beside her signature writes, "and Kov."

She glances up and catches Kov and Mrs. Pelletier exchanging a look that she would swear could be erotic if she didn't know better. She looks again and decides she doesn't know better.

"What should we do with pigeon?"

"He's groggy from the anesthetic, isn't he?"

Mrs. Pelletier peers into the box. "I had a . . ." She stops. "I could keep him here behind the desk," she whispers. Kov nods and gently slides the shoe box across the counter. Lena watches dumbfounded at this bending of the rules.

Outside, they pause at the park gate, and Kov bows slightly when Lena unlocks the iron door and pushes it open. As they stroll the length of the park arm in arm, Kov pauses before the statue of Edwin Booth and says, "O day and night, but this is wondrous strange!"

Lena opens her mouth to match Kov's quote. Remarkably, the words do not come.

"Kov," she says, laughing and clutching his arm, "I can't remember a word of it. I don't have a single quote in my head." She pauses and looks up at the trees, afraid her freedom is fleeting. She can almost feel the voices sweep across the valleys of her brain and recede.

It is morning in Gramercy Park, the time of day for nannies and their charges. The footsteps of others can be heard just beyond the iron gates. But the morning park belongs to the very old, the very young, and, of course, the people they employ.

Two toddlers zigzag along the grass and gravel, watched by two young nannies who sip Snapples and call to the boys, then shake their heads and continue talking. One boy runs behind a boxwood hedge, causing the baby birds to scatter. The bolder boy, built like a small blond tank, runs faster, his crew cut buzzing above the boxwood. A blue ball ejects from the bushes and rolls across the grass.

The little tank picks up a rock and hurls it at the bird, unseen by the nannies on the other side of the hedge. He throws another rock, harder this time.

"Stop!" Lena calls.

The children do not hear, or perhaps already under-stand their privilege enough to know they don't have to listen. The smaller boy steps back and giggles, chubby fingers in his mouth.

"Stop!"

Kov selects two small rocks from the ground near the bench and approaches the boys without a word. The rock thrower is unaware of anything except his prey, calculat-ing now as he watches the birds and carefully tracks their movements. He jiggles the rock in his grubby little hands and suddenly throws it at a bird that stands apart from the others. At the same time, a rock lands softly against the child's butt, and he whirls around, clutching his pants. Kov says nothing but reveals the second rock waiting in his palm. Lena selects a rock, too, and holds it up for the boy to see. The boy takes a step toward them, then recon-siders and swipes his arm angrily in the air. He stomps off to his nanny. Instead of telling her, though, and incrimi-nating himself, he yanks on her hands. The nanny resists and offers a bottle of juice. The boy shakes his head no and pouts, then snatches her hand and bites it.

"Kyle!" the nanny says, grabbing him by the shoul-ders, but he shrugs her off. She walks toward the gate, pulling him by the arm. The second nanny gathers their things from the bench and follows with the other boy. Kyle turns at the gate and sticks out his bright pink tongue at them.

"Spoiled brat," Lena says with great satisfaction, since there are so few times one can say such things out loud.

Kov lowers himself onto the bench, one knobby hand gripping the black iron armrest. A starling pecks the abandoned ball.

"To the victors the spoils."

"Speaking of victors, what happened to Katheryn?"

"We'll see. I expect there will be a lot of scrutiny of her work, once people find out about her sources and methods."

"How would people find out?"

He puts his hand over hers and smiles.

"Kov, you wouldn't leak it. The *Record* will take a beating."

"As you told me once, truth beareth away the victory."

A woman approaches the gate, unlocks the door, and opens it, but before she can enter and lock herself inside, a disheveled man approaches. At first he appears to be begging and lifts his open hands, beseeching. She shakes her head no. She steps inside, holding the door very close. The man says in a loud voice that carries across the park, "I just want to come inside. That's all. Nothing else. I just want to come inside and lay down on a bench."

The woman says something that does not carry, and then closes the door. The man puts his hands through the iron railings; he looks like a prisoner asking to be let back inside.

Kov reaches over and pats Lena's hand, without turning his head to look at her. She looks at his profile, serene, bony, the strong cheekbones and the thin flesh, his eyes watchful.

"I thought I was being erased, that's what I imagined was happening with the transcription. That the recorded words were leaking in through my ears, erasing everything inside me. I know, it's silly, and yet . . ."

He pats her hand again. "What will you do now?"

"I don't know, but it will be better. I'm tired of the secondhand life."

"What about Arlene?" he asks.

"You know how you told me once that obits represent democracy?"

"Where the famous and the unknown meet."

"Right. Well, I've written a brief obit for her. Do you think the *Record* would publish it? Not as a paid death notice; as a regular obit. I know the *Record* obits are reported, are supposed to be newsworthy."

"I'll see that it's published."

"You can do that, Kov?"

He looks slightly affronted. "It will be in tomorrow's paper."

And the next day, it was, exactly as she had written it.

ARLENE LEBOW DIES AT 54

Arlene Lebow, a court reporter, died on July 8, after being mauled by lions at the Bronx Zoo. The police allege that she was in the zoo when it closed and that she swam the moat surrounding the lions' den and entered the animals' area, where she was found dead by zookeepers the next morning.

Ms. Lebow, who was blinded from meningitis at the age of 19, used a dictatype machine for the visually impaired in her work as a court reporter for the New York State Criminal and Family Courts, where she was employed for 20 years.

Ms. Lebow was born in 1949 in Manhattan to Charles and Dorothy Lebow. She is survived by her sister, Ellen Lebow, an English professor and Chaucer scholar. "Arlene did not speak more than necessary," Ellen Lebow said, paraphrasing Chaucer, "and what she did say was said in fullest reverence. She was as patient as Griselda, and like her, she understood the subversive power of silence."

In lieu of flowers, Ellen Lebow requests donations be made in Arlene Lebow's memory to the ASPCA and the Cullen Animal Sanctuary in Hudson, N.Y.

ACKNOWLEDGMENTS

Thank you:

Seth Fishman, Chuck Adams, and everyone at Algonquin

The MacDowell Colony, the Norman Mailer Center, the Barbara Deming Memorial Fund

Lisa Callahan, Greg Curtis, Georgia Deoudes, John Joyce, Janice Maffei, Clare Norins, Greg Rowland, Judy Sternlight, Melanie Trotter, Kyoko Uchida

And, most of all, Desmond Jagmohan

The Transcriptionist

A Note from the Author

*

Questions for Discussion

A NOTE FROM THE AUTHOR

In August 2001, after much restless wandering, I found a job transcribing copy for reporters at the *New York Times*. I would like to look back through my journals and make sense of those days, but in my spiral-bound notebook from that period, the pages after the entry for September 10 are blank. Those were not days of writing. They were not days of fiction.

My memories of that fall are spotty. Mostly, I remember walking the sixty-nine blocks from the *Times* building in midtown to my sublet near Columbia University. It was a surreal time when New Yorkers smiled gently at one another as we passed on the street. The job was so strange, and in those weeks and months so numbing, that I had to walk it off. For a while after the September 11 attacks, I spent the first part of my shift in classifieds, often taking death notices for people who had died in the towers.

I cannot remember how we verified the deaths for the

September 11 notices, but I do remember those dreadful calls of grief. "I'm sorry for your loss," we would say before hanging up and then immediately taking the next obituary call, or sometimes, startlingly, a call about an apartment for sale. In the middle of these death calls a man phoned one evening close to deadline. He wanted to dictate an obituary for his son, who had jumped off the Golden Gate Bridge. The body had not been recovered, and there was no funeral home to call for verification, so we couldn't run the notice. The man was distraught. And finally, all he could think to say was, "But I'm a subscriber."

The weeks passed. The *Times* was still on West Forty-Third Street then, but even in that early twentieth-century building that housed printing presses in the basement, the transcription room was like entering another era. There were televisions with VCRs for recording press conferences or political debates that we transcribed for distribution in the newsroom. There were three recording telephones hooked to Dictaphone machines so we could record and transcribe calls from reporters. They might call from anywhere and for any reason. A foreign reporter might call after she lost Internet access. A local reporter with carpal tunnel might call in to save her wrists. Often, magazine or investigative writers would drop off tapes of long interviews that were later folded into stories or profiles. There were four transcriptionists who worked in shifts, and it seemed our workload was always either too much or not enough. During slow periods, one of my colleagues liked to say, "We're racehorses. They pay us to be ready." A metaphor that made me uncomfortable, especially when my body began to resist the work. I physically recoiled at the daily process of hooking myself to a machine. I would automatically turn my head away as I slipped on the headset, like a horse resisting the bit.

It is still difficult to explain how ravaging I eventually found that job, taking in people's personal tragedies day after day. And the unreality of it, going from a call about a bombing in Kabul to a dance review by Anna Kisselgoff, who always spelled B-a-l-a-n-c-h-i-n-e, every single time. In part it was the passivity of witnessing tragedy, witnessing it with my ears, and serving only as a conduit, what Gay Talese called the reporters' "midwife," passing the news through my body and sending it to be processed into tidy column inches.

My time as an amanuensis ticked by, and I was aware that I was witnessing the end of something: at an immediate level, the end of my department (the transcription room closed in 2007, a few years after I left) and, at a larger level, the decline of newspapers and the turbulent transition to a Web-based news world.

I wasn't able to write about it for a long time. And the way it came out was in fits and fragments, the real meeting the unreal in my notebook, until suddenly a woman

QUESTIONS FOR DISCUSSION

1. During the course of *The Transcriptionist*, Lena, the title character, changes in many ways. What do you see as the most significant change she undergoes, and what kind of person do you think she will be two years after the story ends?

2. In light of Lena's conflicted relationship with the news—with its significance and yet its sometimes messy ethics—how do you view the relationship between the press and democracy? Do we need a traditional press to have an informed public?

3. Is Katheryn Keel, the ambitious but ethically compromised reporter, a good journalist? Are her actions justified—even in part? Why?

4. Lena and Katheryn both make decisions based on their ideas of the best ways to search for truth. Are their actions comparable?

5. The fictional newspaper, the *Record*, serves as a stand-in for newspapers and the press in general. Given the recent developments in technology and the shift in how news is transmitted—including the fact that the job of transcriptionist no longer exists—do you think newspapers will survive? Does it matter? Where will the next generations get their information?

6. The author works for a newspaper. If all novelists write, to some degree at least, from life experiences, do you think anything is or should be off-limits for a fiction writer?

7. A lion and a pigeon play big parts in the novel. What do you view as the function of the animals in the story?

8. In what ways does Lena's background as a minister's daughter and a literature graduate student affect her life and her relationship to language? Do you believe, as one critic states, that the novel "asks whether, in our flooded information age, language can continue to have meaning"? If so, what do you think is the answer?

9. How does Lena's professional life shape the way she thinks about the world around her, and about herself? Why do you believe she chose such lonely work and has endured it for so long?

10. Do you think the surreal quality of life for Lena at the *Record* is a reflection of that environment, or is it an extension of her mental state? Do you believe that an institution such as that newspaper would actually issue gas masks to all its employees, or do you think the author invented this in order to make the place feel more alien?

11. We find out at the end of the novel that Lena's friend Kov is not who he seems. Were you surprised about his true identity, or did you have suspicions?

12. Lena's obsession with the story of the woman who committed suicide led her to violate certain long-standing codes in the newspaper business. Do you feel her actions deserved punishment, or was she innocently trying to help solve a mystery?

13. Recent studies have suggested that following constant news coverage of frightening, emotionally wrenching stories can have negative effects. Do you curb your intake of news because of this? What's the solution, if you believe there is one?

DIANA PAPPAS

Amy Rowland previously worked as a transcriptionist at the *New York Times* and now is an editor for the *New York Times Book Review*. She lives in New York City. This is her first book.